Veronica at the Wells

Lorna Hill wrote her first stories in an exercise book after watching Pavlova dance in Newcastle. Her daughter, Vicki, aged ten, discovered one of these stories and was so delighted by it that Lorna Hill wrote several more and soon they were published. Vicki trained as a ballet dancer at Sadler's Wells and from her letters, Mrs Hill was able to glean the knowledge which forms the background for the 'Wells' stories.

Veronica At The Wells, the second title in the series, takes Veronica back to London to the Sadler's Wells Ballet School where she eventually becomes successful and appears in her first star roles at Covent Garden.

A Dream of Sadler's Wells, Masquerade At The Wells and *No Castanets At The Wells* are also published in Piccolo.

By the same author in Piccolo Books

A DREAM OF SADLER'S WELLS
MASQUERADE AT THE WELLS
NO CASTANETS AT THE WELLS

Veronica at the Wells

LORNA HILL

Illustrated by Kathleen Whapham

A Piccolo Book

PAN BOOKS LTD
LONDON

First published 1951 by Evans Brothers Ltd.
This edition published 1972 by Pan Books Ltd,
33 Tothill Street, London, S.W.1

ISBN 0 330 02900 2

Printed in Great Britain by
Richard Clay (The Chaucer Press), Ltd., Bungay, Suffolk

To Claude Newman, the real 'Gilbert Delahaye', in sincere admiration of his whole-hearted devotion to the art of Ballet

Contents

Chapter 1

The Great Day Arrives

WHEN I woke up that morning, with the autumn sun streaming across my bed, I had the old familiar feeling that something wonderful had happened to me. For several days now I'd had that feeling, and, as I lay there, it suddenly burst upon me what it was that had happened. I'd had my audition, and had been accepted for that most romantic of all schools – the Sadler's Wells Ballet School!

Then the wonderful top-of-the-world feeling changed to a fluttering in my inside – the sort of feeling you get when you jump into the swimming bath for the first time in the season or go on the scenic railway. It was a feeling partly of excitement, partly joy, but most of all apprehension, because today was THE DAY! Yes, this very morning, in less than two hours' time, I'd be walking up to the porticoed building that said 45 Colet Gardens on a brass plate by the side of the door, and from that moment I'd be a member of the most famous dancing school in the world. No wonder I felt excited!

I jumped out of bed and ran over to a chair whereon stood a small attaché-case, opened it, and peeped inside. Yes, everything was there – the new, grey silk tunic (oh, the awful job I'd had to get it made in time!), pink tights, belt, and matching hairband, blocked and unblocked shoes. I'd even remembered to put in hairgrips and a hairnet. I couldn't help giggling when I thought of the things you usually take to a new school with you – things like fountain pens and india-rubbers! On top of everything was a note from the secretary, telling me how to get to Colet Gardens. I'd put it in because it was sweet of her to think of it, but really there was no need for it – the locality of the school was written on my heart!

I washed and dressed quicker than I had ever done in my life before, and flew to the door.

'Mrs Crapper! Mrs Crapper!' I yelled down the stairs. 'Is my breakfast ready, Mrs Crapper? I've got to be there before ten o'clock, you know!'

Mrs Crapper, who kept the apartment house where I lived and who had looked after me since Daddy died, came to the foot of the stairs and stood looking up at me, her hands on her hips.

'Lawks, Miss Veronica! Why, it's barely half past seven! But I knew as how you'd be up with the lark this mornin', and your kipper's in the pan. I've just turned it over this very minute, and it'll be done in a trice.'

'Don't bring my breakfast up here, Mrs Crapper,' I shouted back. 'I'll come down there and have it with you – honestly, I'd rather.'

I thought how shocked Aunt June would be. Aunt June had made all arrangements for Mrs Crapper to look after me. I was to have my own bedroom and share a sitting-room with another ballet student, and we were to have our meals brought up to us in state. Instead, we usually had them in Mrs Crapper's basement kitchen, where we could make toast at her open fire – much more homely!

I finished my toilet, made my bed, shut my case, and then put on my outdoor things so that I shouldn't have to come back to my room again after I'd finished my breakfast. At the door I paused and looked back. I suppose it was really a shabby room, but I'd always been happy there. So, although the floor was covered with cheap canvas of a hideous green-and-yellow shade, the bedstead a cheap iron one, and the wall-paper faded to an indiscriminate rust colour, yet I loved the room because I loved Mrs Crapper, and she'd put all her most precious possessions in it for me, The painted dressing-table with all its little drawers for your hairpins and buttons, the thing that Mrs Crapper called an 'overmantel' and which consisted of a lot of little brackets with bits of looking-glass above them, yes, even the very curtains, were the identical furnishings which Mrs Crapper had bought when she was married. And as that had been over thirty years ago you really couldn't blame them for looking a bit the worse for wear! Mrs Crapper assured me that they'd been lovely when they were new, and I quite believed her. On the brackets of the over-mantel stood a proud array of coronation mugs, collected by Mrs Crapper from various members of her family, together with several souvenirs of her honeymoon – a jug with 'A Present From Margate' on it; a teapot with a spout made in the form of a mermaid, and which wouldn't pour out because I'd tried it with water out of my toothmug; and a much-gilded flower vase with 'Margate Remembers You' in flowing letters on its bulging middle.

As I dashed down the three flights of stairs to the basement I passed the closed bedroom door of my fellow ballet student, Stella Mason. How I wished she'd been there to take me to school on my first morning! But she was on tour with the Opera Ballet and wouldn't be back till tonight, so it was no use wishing.

I ate my kipper dutifully when Mrs Crapper put it in front of me, but, really, when I'd finished I couldn't have told you what I'd eaten. My thoughts were far away from Mrs Crapper's basement kitchen. They had flown ahead of me, and were already at Colet Gardens.

'Lawks, Miss Veronica!' exclaimed Mrs Crapper when I got up from the table. 'You'll never be able to dance on what you've eaten for your breakfast. Only a kipper, neat, as you might say! No bread and butter at all, and not even your usual toast and marmalade. All this bally's gone to your head; it has that!'

She insisted upon making me up a huge packet of sand-wiches to sustain me in the middle of the morning. In vain I tried to explain to her about the canteen at the Wells, and the milk so thoughtfully provided by the Government for students under eighteen, but it was no good. She didn't give *that*, she said with a snap of her fingers, for them canteens. As like as not they'd have nothing but lemonade and biscuits! I took the sandwiches because I wouldn't hurt Mrs Crapper's feelings for the world, but since both my case and my handbag were full to bursting, I had to unwrap them when I got safely outside the kitchen and do them up again in two smaller packets. I crammed one in each pocket of my coat, where they stuck out on either side and made me look like an old-fashioned shepherdess with panniers!

I suppose to the ordinary person the journey by Underground to Baron's Court, which is the nearest station to Colet Gardens, is a long and dreary one. But to me it was like the journey to Fairyland. Every rattle of the train, every lurch and every bump, brought me nearer to my heart's desire. A little man in a bowler hat apologized politely as the train swung round a corner, and flung him against my shoulder.

I murmured: 'It's quite all right. It wasn't your fault really,' when all the time I wanted to say: 'Do you know who I am? I'm Veronica Weston, and I'm just about to become a pupil of the Sadler's Wells Ballet School. I'm going to be famous like Margot Fonteyn and Moira Shearer!'

I wanted to turn *fouettés* down the middle of the carriage. I wanted to pose *en arabesque* in the entry every time the train stopped at a station. I thought how surprised they'd be if I did! Then I caught sight of my reflection in the window opposite. Alas! They would never believe me! In my navy-blue reefer coat and beret, chosen for me by Aunt June as suitable wearing apparel for a person only just fifteen, I looked much more like a schoolgirl than a glamorous ballet dancer. In fact – I have to admit it – my small pale face looked a great deal younger than fifteen.

It was exactly nine-twenty by the clock of St Paul's School when I reached the door of 45 Colet Gardens – the fateful door! Girls, and quite a lot of boys too, were pouring through a door that led into what looked like nothing so much as a greenhouse. I stayed for quite a long time outside, trying to screw up my courage to follow them. When at last I did so I found myself in a big, light room rather like a conservatory. There were little green tables dotted about, with green chairs to match. The chairs were of the modern, tubular type, and they looked as if they'd collapse if you sat down on them, but I found out that they were very strong really. They had to be, because they weren't exactly gently treated! Two girls, one fair, the other dark, were standing by a radiator looking at a notice-board that hung on the wall above.

'Golly! Myrna's got an understudy for a Court Lady in *Lac*. What an honour – I *don't* think!' said the dark girl. 'Theo and Linda are Pages. Delia's got one of the Nymphs in *Sleeping Prin*, and Mary's an understudy. Oh, and she's one of the Pages as well. You know – the ones with the ghastly violins in the First Act. I'm on the other list – one of the Black Lackeys in *The Gods Go A-Begging*, down at the Wells. Oh, well, it'll be a change from Covent Garden, anyway! Nothing for you, Pauline ... *Well?*' This last exclamation was due to the fact of my having plucked her by the sleeve.

'Please, would you mind telling me where the dressing-rooms are?' I asked.

The girl stared at me witheringly. Then she jerked her head nonchalantly towards a passageway and said :

'Through there. Down the passage, on your right. Don't knock.' Then she turned her back on me.

I followed her directions, and approached a closed door from behind which I could hear the confused hum of voices. When I opened it I found, to my amazement, that it was full of boys and young men. A burst of laughter from the Winter Garden told me without more explanation that I had been made a fool of.

I retreated hastily, my cheeks burning. Then, as I stood, not knowing which way to go, I felt a touch on my arm.

'Here – come this way, if you please.'

I turned and found myself facing a dark boy wearing a pair of very old flannel slacks and a grey pullover. He wasn't good-looking in the ordinary sense of the word, but he had kind, brown eyes and he looked friendly.

'I – I'm most awfully sorry,' I stammered. 'I mean, barging in among you all like that. You see, I didn't know—'

'Do not apologize,' said the boy, and then I noticed that he spoke with a foreign accent. 'It was obviously a mistake. We all knew it, of course. The girls' dressing-room is over there.' He indicated a short flight of stone stairs with a door at the bottom. 'If you need any more help, ask me, please. The name is Toni.'

'Thank you so much,' I answered. 'I'll be all right now, I expect.'

The door of the girls' dressing-room was ajar, and above the general chatter of voices I could hear snatches of conversation.

'It's a fine thing when I have to be understudy to Delia McFarlane! Why, she's the world's worst!' ... 'Don't worry, darling; nothing will happen to Delia; she's the world's healthiest, besides being the worst.' ... 'No, I haven't seen your tights, Lily. I expect they're in the lost prop, as usual. I can't think why you *will* keep on leaving them on the floor. Hey! Has anyone seen Lily's tights? Colour pink once upon a time; now a delicate grey – something like Mrs Wopping's floorcloth.' ... 'Whoever gave you your name, Lily, was playing a joke. Anything less like a lily than you in your tights no one ever saw!' ... 'Sorry, I can't lend you mine. Oh, yes, I know I haven't a class till three o'clock, but these are the only decent pair I possess, and you'd split them.' ... '*Belinda!* Why don't you get properly dressed? It looks awful dancing *Les Sylphides* in your undies!'

At this point I entered. The voices ceased as if they'd been cut off at the main like the water, and thirty to forty pairs of eyes were turned on me curiously.

'I – I was told to come in here,' I said tentatively.

'Oh, new, I suppose?' said a fair girl standing near the door.

14

She had a small, round face, and her lint-fair hair was tightly plaited and pinned on top of her head. It gave her an odd look, as if she was going to have a bath. 'Well, we've all got to be new some time, haven't we? Cheer up, and don't look so scared! You'll soon drop into things.'

'You will find a peg over on the other side,' put in another girl. She was dark-skinned and spoke with a slight foreign accent. I found out in due course that her name was Taiis (pronounced Ty-eece) Sircar, and that she had been the cause of great embarrassment to poor Miss Smailes who taught in the Junior School where Taiis had been training until a year ago. Miss Smailes had been explaining to the class that they ought not to behave like a herd of unruly school-children.

'You ought to make believe that you are all little princesses,' said Miss Smailes, 'and carry yourselves accordingly.'

She hadn't realized until some time afterwards that Taiis, one of the worst offenders, *was* in fact a princess in her own country! Incidentally, she was one of the gentlest girls I met while I was at the Wells, and the least regal in the ordinary sense of the word.

'Thank you,' I said gratefully, glad that they were not all as unfriendly as the girl I had addressed in the Winter Garden when I'd first come in. As a matter of fact I'd had a spot of beginner's luck in reverse on that occasion. Marcia Rutherford was quite the nastiest girl at the Wells; in fact, she was the only really objectionable one I met while I was there.

The girl who'd been dancing twirled her imaginary skirts.

'Bet you I dare dance round the Winter Garden!' she announced to the room in general.

There was a gasp of horror.

'What? Like that? *Belinda!* Why, you might meet Gilbert Delahaye, or Serge, or – or even the *Director*!'

'What odds! Cheer the old boy up a bit!'

The girl with the plaits, whose name appeared to be Sara, planted herself firmly in front of the door.

15

'Oh, no you don't, Belinda!' she pronounced. 'You know what they said in your report.'

'SHE MUST LEARN TO BEHAVE WITH DECORUM!' chanted a dozen voices.

'The Director's frightfully keen on Decorum,' went on Sara. 'It'll be written on his heart when he dies! I do hope you're decorous, New Girl.'

'I hope so!' I laughed.

'I can't *think* why they took you into this ballet school, Belinda,' pursued Sara. 'It's so strict here – tradition, and all that, don't you know. Such and such a thing was never done in the Russian Imperial Ballet School – *never*! And so it can't be done here. It's really terribly straitlaced, and you're so – so – well, sometimes you're not very decent, you know.'

'I really don't know what you're all so shocked about,' declared Belinda. 'Personally, I think I look rather nice.'

I stared at her thoughtfully. 'Rather nice?' It didn't describe her in the very least. She was completely beautiful from the crown of her red-gold head to her slender white feet. And yet there was something – something you couldn't quite put your finger on – that spoilt her. I'd discussed it with Sara one day when I'd been at the Wells for some time.

'I think it's because her thoughts aren't nice ones,' I said. 'Madame says that if your thoughts aren't nice, it shows in your dancing, just as it does in music or painting.'

'Madame who?' questioned Sara.

'Madame Viret – where I used to learn dancing,' I explained. 'She has a studio in Baker Street.'

'Oh, yes – I've heard of the Wakulski-Viret School, of course,' said Sara. 'Everyone has. Madame Viret's a wonderful teacher, isn't she?'

'Absolutely wonderful,' I answered. 'Well, Madame says that if you're like – well, like Belinda is, you'll get three-quarters of the way to the top – perhaps even to solo parts – but you'll never get *right* there, because your mind will stop you, no matter how brilliantly you dance.'

'She's right,' said Sara, after a minute's thought. 'I never thought of it like that, but it's perfectly true.'

But to get back to the dressing-room. Belinda had now sobered up a bit, and was shrugging herself into her grey silk tunic.

'I suppose you haven't come here with a scholarship?' she asked, smoothing it down over her lovely slender figure, and addressing me.

'Well, yes – as a matter of fact I have,' I admitted.

'Oh!—' The whole dressing-room was suddenly alive with attention. 'A whole one, or only a bit of one?'

'A whole one, I suppose,' I answered, 'At least, I don't have to pay any fees, but of course there are my lodgings, and everything.'

'I get more out of them than that,' put in Belinda, doing high kicks to the danger of all around her. 'They pay all my fees, *and* give me something towards my keep as well. They even pay for my lunches. They know they jolly well have to, or I wouldn't be here. My dad is out of work, and likely to be. He's like me, is Dad – bone lazy! Mum does part-time in a shoe factory, but she's got veins in her legs with standing, and she may go sick any day. Well, what Mum gets is all the cash we have coming into our house, and there are ten of us.' She began to recite the names and ages of her family, ticking them off on her slim, white fingers: 'Doug, Maisie, Walt, Mabel, Ernie, Ruth, Willie. Then there's Alfie – he's ten, and he's got TB. He's in a Home, so that's got rid of *him* for a bit, thank goodness! Oh, and there's Gertie – I nearly forgot about Gertie. Let me see, she must be six; or is it seven? I can't remember. Anyway, she can't walk, poor kid – infantile paralysis. Well, I think that's the lot. Personally I consider I deserve a scholarship! They threatened to stop it at the end of last term, after that row Derek and I got into, but I knew they wouldn't. I'm far too good a dancer.' She began turning *pirouettes* – trebles, and even fours, and they were so wonderful that I couldn't help gasping. 'I parked myself outside the

17

staff-room door,' she went on, 'when I knew they were having a pow-wow, and I pretended to be talking to a friend, and I said in a loud voice, so that they simply couldn't *help* hearing, "OK," I said, "if they stop my schol, I'm going straight to the Windmill. *They'll* have me like a shot." ... I knew my schol wouldn't be stopped, and it hasn't. They like a bit of temperament in this place, anyway,' she added, stopping in the middle of a *pirouette* and throwing back her hair. 'How's this for *entrechat-six*?' She jumped into the air and seemed to stay there for ages, while her slender feet twinkled. 'Good enough even for Gilbert, eh?' She gave her tights a last hitch and danced away.

'Hey!' yelled Sara after her flying figure. 'You've forgotten your hair!'

'Oh, I'll come back later on to do it up,' shouted Belinda. 'Only practising, now. Thanks, though!'

'She's quite a decent sort,' remarked Sara when she'd gone. 'Really, you can't help liking her. If only she wasn't so – so—'

'We know what you mean, darling!' laughed a girl called Margaret. 'It's a bit difficult to describe, I'll admit. For myself, I certainly shouldn't call Belinda Stout a "decent sort". Fascinating and scintillating is more like it! She's got oceans of personality, and lashings of sparkle, but not one ounce of ordinary common or garden decency. But she'll be in the Company before any of us staid people. You'll see!'

'Yes – if she doesn't go just a bit *too* far,' said Sara. 'As I said before, it's a wonder to me why they keep her in this school. In my opinion it's touch and go with Belinda.'

'Oh, I think she's safe enough,' argued Margaret. 'They can't afford to turn out anyone who can dance like Belinda.'

'You never can tell,' put in Marcia, giving me a sidelong look which showed that she disliked me just as much as I disliked her. 'A scholarship means nothing. Remember Patsy, that pale-faced girl who came here with a schol, flags flying and the band playing? Everyone thought she'd be in the Company, and into solo parts in a twink. And in less than a year she was turned out. She went into another company – I forget which.' She yawned loudly.

'The European,' supplied Sara, who seemed to be a positive well of information. 'And there was a reason for her being turned out, you know. Her thighs got too big, and of course for a company like the Sadler's Wells Ballet your figure's got to be perfect as well as your dancing. Incidentally, I read about her in some magazine or other, and she seems to be doing quite well. I'm glad – she was quite a decent sort.'

Marcia shrugged her shoulders.

'You and your decent sorts! She had no pep. Not a bit of good for the Ballet.'

'Oh, I don't know,' argued Sara. 'What about Beryl Grey? You couldn't call *her* exactly peppy, and she's ever so nice. Why, she even kissed me the night I gave her that bunch of willowherb I gathered off the wasteland near Cadby Hall. *Some* people would have been frightfully sniffy, but *she* wasn't. She knew that I hadn't any money to buy her real flowers. By the way, I've still got the bit of cottonwool I rubbed the greasepaint off with where she kissed me. I'm saving it for an heirloom to hand on to my grandchildren!'

'By the way,' put in the dark-skinned Taiis half-apologetically to me, 'you do not need to put on your tights and tunic just yet, you know. The Continuation classes come before our dancing.'

'Yes – English and French, and all that rot,' said Marcia. 'Waste of time, I call it!'

'Must be well educated to be a good dancer,' said Sara briskly. 'The Director says so, and so does Madame, and I expect they're quite right, even if it does seem a bit hard to us to have to stodge French verbs when we might be dancing.'

'But Belinda—' I said, thinking of the Titian-haired girl dancing off in her tights and tunic.

'Oh, Belinda cuts most of the Continuation classes,' said Sara with a shrug. 'But *you* mustn't do it. Come on!'

Chapter 2

Gilbert

My first morning passed like a dream. Before I knew it, the English lesson was over and there was an interval for milk and biscuits. After this we had French, and then a longer interval before afternoon school, when most of the dancing classes were held. I had lunch at school, and I may say that it was an excellent meal.

'Too good!' laughed Sara, who was sitting next to me. 'According to Gilbert, that is! Gilbert, by the way, is Mr Gilbert Delahaye who takes most of our classes. He's English, in spite of his name and the way he behaves.'

'What do you mean – "the way he behaves"?' I asked curiously.

Sara laughed.

'He's what you might call temperamental. He shouts, and bangs his stick on the floor and on the *barre*, and sometimes you imagine he's going to attack *you*, but of course he never does; he's a lamb really, and most awfully popular with everybody. The Senior class is wild with jealousy because we have Gilbert. Well, as I say, he positively *raves* about the lunches.'

Wickedly Sara propped her elbows on the table and mimicked Gilbert in his fury:

'What on earth have you girls been eating? Suet pudding again! Well, I must say, you certainly dance like it! Really, it's absurd to expect a ballet dancer to execute *entrechats-six* on four helpings of suet pudding! Now, come along! There must be *some* of you who have not feasted on suet pudding! . . .'

After Sara's vivid description, I stared curiously at Mr Gilbert Delahaye – by the way, he pronounced it 'Dellerhaye'

– when I entered the Baylis Hall for my first class with him. At first sight he had public school and 'varsity written all over him. He might have been a rowing blue, or a county cricketer, or indeed any sort of athlete. He certainly wasn't the least bit like the traditional dancing master – not in appearance, anyway. But appearances are sometimes deceptive, and it was so in Gilbert's case. He'd been a famous dancer, and he had all the well-known characteristics hidden under that old-school-tie exterior. Artistic temperament, flow of sarcasm, generosity of nature. All dancers aren't generous, but most really great ones are. Gilbert Delahaye was known to have helped many a struggling student by giving him free coaching and encouraging him generally.

Well, as I say, Gilbert would enter the room, mount the platform, polished of manner, calm of eye. In less than ten minutes, however, he would have shed his restraint, together with most or all of his pullovers – he often wore several – and would be striding up and down the room, banging his stick and delivering a continuous stream of sarcastic remarks. In fact, he would behave in such a temperamental way that it was indeed hard to believe that he really *was* English. I came to the conclusion, when I had been at the Wells for a short time, that most of it was a pose to make us work, and, if so, it certainly succeeded. We adored him – the boys especially – and slackness in his classes was unknown. Incidentally, he worked harder than anybody, and at the end of the day he would have put so much into his teaching that he was quite exhausted himself.

At the end of this first class, after we had made our curtsies, he mopped his damp forehead with a silk handkerchief that he kept expressly for the purpose, and motioned me to stay behind the rest.

'You're new, aren't you?' he said. 'Ah, yes – I remember now – I barged into your audition, didn't I? I knew I'd seen you somewhere before. Where were you trained – Wakulski-Viret, I suppose?'

'Yes,' I answered in astonishment. 'However did you know?'

He laughed.

'Oh, by certain characteristics – little movements of the head and hands that Madame Viret passes on to her students. Oh, don't look so dismayed – they're not *bad* characteristics! On the contrary, they're good ones. Madame Viret is a wonderful teacher – one of the best in the world.'

I nodded.

'Yes – it's marvellous just to watch her move,' I said. 'I began learning from her when I was ten, and I've never been anywhere else, except for last year when I went to live with my cousins in Northumberland. While I was there I went to a dancing school in Newcastle – a Miss Martin was the head of it. She was wonderful, too.'

To my surprise Gilbert seemed to know all about Miss Martin.

'Ah, yes,' he said. 'Another excellent teacher. Well, with all that behind you, you've certainly got something to live up to! You've got a nice "line", you know. By the way – your name?'

I told him my name, and he dismissed me with a smile. As I went out of the Baylis Hall I nearly had a head-on collision with Marcia Rutherford. It was quite obvious that she'd been listening outside the door, and I wondered how much she'd heard. By the expression on her face, as she looked at me, I knew that she'd caught Gilbert's last remark, and with a queer feeling in my heart I knew also that Marcia Rutherford was my enemy.

As I went home by the Underground that night after school, my thoughts were very different to those I had had when I'd travelled in the opposite direction that morning. No longer did I ache to turn *pirouettes* down the centre of the compartment, or to pose *en arabesque* in the entry. For one thing, I was much too tired, and for another I had had a good deal of the self-conceit knocked out of me during my first few classes at the Wells. I wasn't so sure, now, that my *pirouettes* were so very good, after all – not after seeing Belinda's! I didn't feel that my *arabesque* was as perfect as I had always believed it to be. I lived again in my mind the classes I had attended that first day at the Wells – the Ballet, Character, and Elementary Mime – and to be quite frank, I hadn't received the attention I'd expected. Apart from Gilbert, who'd been kind and asked me where I'd been trained, no one else had taken the least notice of me. I don't believe that Serge Lopokoff, the Russian dancing master, who'd taken the Character class, had even *seen* me, as I manfully struggled with new steps in the back row, let alone been dazzled by my brilliance. If it hadn't been for Toni Rossini, who'd came forward and offered to be my partner and had helped me all he could, I'd have been hopelessly out of my depth. Yes, Serge Lopokoff hadn't been very helpful. Still, I liked the gentle little man with his exquisite hands and his mild blue eyes that had a far-away expression in them, as if his thoughts had strayed back again to the Leningrad school where he was trained.

As the train rumbled along I couldn't help smiling to myself and thinking how utterly unlike a temperamental Russian dancing master Serge Lopokoff was.

I hadn't fared any better at the Mime class either. Everyone knew more than I did, for I hadn't learnt any Classical Mime at Madame Viret's or at Miss Martin's. It took me all my time to manage the gestures 'I' and 'you' correctly. I consoled myself with the thought that, if you could go by what you read, Margot Fonteyn hadn't been noticed at first either – not outwardly, anyway. 'Perhaps,' I said to myself, 'they're watching me all the time, although they don't show it. Anyhow, they'll jolly well *have* to before long, because I mean to work and work, even if I have to do it in the backest of back rows!'

The train got fuller and fuller, and I stood up to let an old lady, who carried two enormous brown-paper parcels, have my seat. After all, if I *had* been on my feet all day, so probably

23

had she, and she was quite three times my age. Two outsize businessmen hung on straps on either side of me and talked racing over my head. I felt in danger of being squashed any minute! I looked at my wristwatch and saw that it was half past five already. Mrs Crapper would have finished her tea long ago, but I hoped that Jonathan would have waited for me, so that we could have it together in Mrs Crapper's kitchen.

I don't think I've told you about Jonathan, have I? He was an artist and he lived on the top floor of Mrs Crapper's apartment house. The top floor was really one large attic, with two smaller ones opening off it. Jonathan used the smaller attics for his bedroom and kitchen. The big attic was his studio, and Jonathan said that, now he'd had the big skylight put in the roof, it suited him down to the ground – if you can say that about an attic!

Jonathan was enormous – over six feet tall, and broad in proportion. He had curly black hair, brilliant dark eyes, and a little black beard. He was really quite young – about twenty-six – although he looked older because of the beard. In spite of being so big and strong, you couldn't have met a gentler person than Jonathan. Not even the kitten that used to climb in from the next-door attic and rub itself against his legs, nor the little grey mouse busily picking up stray crumbs from his floor; not even the spider that had the temerity to spin a web over the top corner of his easel had anything to fear from Jonathan.

'They have as much right to live on the earth as I have,' he'd say, as he put a bluebottle carefully out of the window. 'Why should I believe that the sun only shines for me?'

'You wait till your meat gets fly-blown, Mr Jonathan,' put in Mrs Crapper, sensible as ever. 'Then you'll think different. You will that!'

'I don't eat meat,' Jonathan answered with a flash of his white teeth. 'Surely you know that by now, Martha! I'm a vegetarian.'

'Yes, I *do* know it, Mr Jonathan,' said Mrs Crapper

severely. 'And it ain't right, that's what I says, that a great strapping fellow like you should be living on lettuces and tomatoes and suchlike bits of things. It ain't nat'ral. You'll be fading away before long, I shouldn't wonder!'

Jonathan said no more. I think that Mrs Crapper's logic, or rather the lack of it, was beyond him!

Besides Jonathan, several other people lived in Mrs Crapper's apartment house. There was a middle-aged woman who was secretary to a corset manufacturer. Her name was Broadbent, and she was very straightlaced – perhaps her job had got the better of her! I'm pretty sure she didn't really approve of the rest of us. The 'rest' comprised a girl named Miriam Samuels. She was dark, pretty, and very vivacious. She was a dancing student at a stage school, and she'd shared a room with Stella Mason, the ballet student I told you about before, until a few weeks ago when a talent scout had spotted her. Now she was at the Windmill Theatre, and doing well. She'd left Mrs Crapper's so as to be nearer her job.

The deep rumbling voices of the two large businessmen kept breaking in upon my thoughts. They had stopped talking about horses and were now discussing somebody's preference shares, and why they were a good thing, and why George had parted with somebody else's ordinaries, and that a slump was bound to come, didn't George think so? I couldn't help thinking what funny things men are interested in!

At last the welcome words 'Chalk Farm' slid past the window, and I fought my way out. I got a bus the rest of the way, but of course I had to wait for it, so it was well after six o'clock by the time I found myself walking down the long row of houses called – ironically enough! – Heather Hill, where Mrs Crapper's apartment house was. Unluckily, No 242 was at the opposite end of the road to the bus stop! It seemed years and years since I had left it this morning, and really it was almost impossible to believe that the sun, which had shone down on me out of the cold eastern sky this morning, was only just now setting in a flurry of pink cloud behind the laburnum tree in the garden opposite. I felt that at least a week of sunrises and sunsets had passed since I had set out on my great adventure.

I ran down the basement stairs to Mrs Crapper's kitchen, but the room was empty, although there was a beautiful coal fire roaring in the grate. My heart gave a throb of disappointment. But, of course, both Mrs Crapper and Jonathan would have finished tea long ago. Why, it was nearly time for supper!

I left the cosy kitchen with a sigh of regret, and toiled slowly up the three long flights of stairs to my own room. I noticed, just as I had done when I'd come back from Northumberland, the strong smell of carbolic soap, wet wood, and boiled cabbage that hung over the house – especially the bottom half. I must say that, when you got to Jonathan's top floor, the smell was drowned by the more pungent one of oil paint and turpentine!

When I reached my own room I switched on the light and looked round. My tea was on the table, and there was a note beside it which said: 'Mind you make a reel good tea ave gon round to the shop for tin of beans and pkt soap powder back in a jiffy martha crapper.' Other than this, everything was exactly as I had left it when I'd dashed out this morning – even to a pair of tights on the table with the darning needle sticking in them. It was quite evident that Stella hadn't got back from her tour yet.

Chapter 3

Stella

I TOOK off my outdoor things, made myself some cocoa on the gas-ring, and sat down to my belated tea. I had just finished, and was wondering what to do until suppertime – mend my tights or darn a new pair of practice shoes – when my eye caught sight of an orange envelope propped against the tea-caddy. I expect that Mrs Crapper, being tea-minded, had put it there thinking I couldn't possibly miss it. She hadn't thought about cocoa!

The telegram was from Aunt June, and I've often wondered since what on earth the post-office authorities must have thought about it. It said:

CAN REMEMBER ONLY WHOOPING-COUGH. PLEASE WIRE OTHER DISEASES. AUNT JUNE.

Of course! I'd sent the health certificate and other forms from the school on to poor Aunt June, quite forgetting that she couldn't possibly know what infectious diseases I'd had, since I'd only lived with her for about a year. Evidently I'd told her about the whooping-cough at some time or other, and that was how she knew about it.

The wire was prepaid, so I hastily scribbled on the reply form:

SCARLET FEVER. MUMPS. CHICKEN-POX TWICE. MEASLES NOT SURE. LOVE VERONICA.

I had just finished, and was putting on my hat and coat again to go out to the post office, when there was a footstep on the stairs – a footstep that certainly didn't belong to Mrs Crapper who clamped, or Jonathan who bounded.

'Stella!' I yelled.

'Yes, it's me,' said Stella's well-known voice. 'Hullo, Veronica! Gosh! It's wonderful to see you again. You haven't altered much either – except that you aren't so pale, and you aren't skinny any more.'

'*You've* altered lots,' I said. 'Why, you're quite grown up!'

'I'm eighteen,' laughed Stella. 'I don't feel a bit like it sometimes. Golly! How time flies!'

I looked at Stella as she took off her coat and hat, and thought how pretty she'd grown. She had soft, fair hair that waved naturally; it was shoulder-length, as every ballet dancer's hair must be, and it was turned under in a simple page-boy style. Her face was heart shaped, and she had a lovely creamy complexion that needed no powder or cream to make it look like the petal of a flower. Then I noticed that she was looking tired. Her soft, generous mouth drooped a little at the corners, and there were violet shadows under her eyes.

'Stella, you've been slimming?' I said severely. Although Stella was three years older than I was, I always 'mothered' her. There was something about Stella that made you want to take care of her. 'Have you been going without your meals?'

'No, I haven't – honestly,' said Stella. 'I've had jolly good breakfasts, and – and suppers. I have, really, Veronica. I expect I look tired because I've been travelling all night.'

'What about your lunches?' I persisted. 'Have you been skipping them?'

'Just a few,' Stella admitted guiltily. 'But not because I'm slimming, though I *am* getting horribly fat, but because lunches are so expensive. Two shillings a lunch – it mounts up.'

'But I always thought you got paid the earth in the Opera Ballet – more than in the real ballet!' I exclaimed.

'Oh, the pay is quite good,' said Stella. 'But you see, since Granny was ill I've been sending home as much as I possibly could for her to get someone to help her in the house and to do her washing for her, and so on. She's getting old, you know; she's over eighty. By the way, there aren't any letters for me, are there? I haven't heard from Granny all this week.'

'There are no letters for you,' I answered. Then I was about to explain about Aunt June and her funny wire, when Stella saw the orange envelope lying on the table.

'Oh, Veronica,' she said in a strange far-off voice. 'The telegram? Is it for me? ... Granny ...'

'Oh, no!' I laughed. 'It's from Aunt June, and guess what she says? She wants to know – why, what's the matter, Stella?'

Stella's little heart-shaped face seemed to have grown even smaller and whiter. She swayed a little as she stood.

'Oh, Veronica – I – feel so funny,' she whispered.

Then, to my horror, she crumpled up at my feet in a dead faint.

'Jonathan!' I shrieked, rushing to the door. 'Mrs Crapper – Jonathan! Come quickly! – Oh, Jonathan!'

They both came running – Mrs Crapper had evidently got back from her shopping – but Jonathan was there first. He came tumbling down his attic stairs like a thunderbolt.

'What is it, Veronica? What's the matter?' Then he saw Stella lying at my feet, and his face went white.

'Oh, Jonathan!' I sobbed. 'Is she dead? Do you think she's dead?'

Jonathan looked up – he'd gone down on his knees beside Stella, and was chafing her hands.

'Dead? Good Lord, no! She's just fainted, that's all. Get a spot of brandy, Martha, there's a good soul. There's some in the cupboard in my bedroom.' He lifted Stella up as if she were a baby – and indeed she was, compared to him – and propped her in a chair by the window which he'd already opened. 'She's coming round. Put the kettle on, Veronica, and

29

get her a cup of something hot to drink. I suspect she's been living on tea and buns. She feels like it!'

After she'd sipped the brandy that Mrs Crapper brought, Stella revived very quickly. She drank the tea that I made, and Jonathan fed her like a baby with strips of toast dipped in the hot liquid.

'No dancing for you tomorrow,' he pronounced, when the colour had come back into her cheeks. 'Bed for you, my child, and no nonsense. I'll bring you your meals myself.'

'Oh, but I couldn't do that,' protested Stella. 'I'm supposed to be in class as usual tomorrow morning.'

'If you don't do as you're told,' threatened Jonathan, 'I shall ring up that confounded school and tell them you fainted—'

'Oh, *no*, Jonathan!' cried Stella, 'No, *please*! They'll say—'

'They'll say that this dancing business is too much for you,' said Jonathan. 'And they won't be far wrong either.' He looked down at her anxiously. 'What do you want to go on doing it for?'

'Why, Jonathan, it's my *life*!' cried Stella. 'It's the only life for me. I'd die if I didn't dance! Anyway, why all the fuss? Veronica's doing it.'

'Veronica's tough,' pronounced Jonathan. 'If she likes to be mug enough to dedicate her whole life to a stupid thing like ballet, well, it's her own affair.'

'It's *my* own affair too,' argued Stella.

'No, it isn't – not when you frighten the life out of – of people by fainting away like that. It's not your own affair at all. You're not strong enough to do it. Veronica's a chirpy Cockney. You're – you're just a North-Country primrose.'

'I always thought that North-Country people were tough as tough,' I put in. 'The Director said so at my audition. And anyway, *I'm* partly North Country. My mother was Aunt June's sister, and she came from Northumberland.'

'I give it up!' said Jonathan. 'I always regarded you as one hundred per cent Cockney, Veronica. Let's not argue about it, anyhow. Let's roast chestnuts. I got a bag this morning. Here they are.' He delved beneath his overall into one of his capacious pockets and brought forth a brown-paper bag. 'Now we'll see who's going to be rich. This one is Stella's; this one Veronica's, and the little one is mine.' He placed them carefully in front of the gas-fire. 'Now for the pops! The first one to go off is going to be rich; the second is going to be loved; the third is going to be the successful one – in the eyes of the world, that is!'

We waited for a long time, but nothing happened. Then we forgot about them and began to talk. Jonathan was just telling us about his latest picture – the one of Covent Garden Market – when there was a loud explosion.

'It's yours, Jonathan!' I yelled. 'You're going to be rich. Golly! It's Stella's too – a dead heat! How funny! So you're *both* going to be rich, and you're both going to be loved as well. And it looks as if I'm going to have all the success.'

'Of *course* it's true,' pronounced Jonathan. 'I've always found chestnuts to be most reliable. Naturally, Stella will be loved. No one could possibly help loving Stella.'

Yes, that was certainly true, I thought. Stella was very gentle and sweet. She hadn't an unkind or an ungenerous thought in her head, and she was as pretty as she was good.

'What about me?' I demanded, pretending to be annoyed. 'Isn't there a bit of love left over for me?'

'Not a spot!' said Jonathan, striking an attitude. Incidentally, he looked magnificent, standing there drawn up to his full height. 'You, Veronica, cast aside the flower of love for the tinsel blossom of fame. What more do you want?'

'I think I'd like a little bit of love as well, please – if you don't mind,' I said meekly.

'Don't be greedy, Veronica! You can't have both,' said Jonathan flatly. 'Not in the world of ballet, anyway. It's either love or fame; you've only to see that well-known film – what's its name? – to learn that. If you flirt with both, you come to a messy end!' He spoke so seriously that I stared at him. But he was looking down at Stella with the strangest expression in his dark eyes, and really it was just as if he was addressing *her*, and not me at all, so I said no more.

After a while Jonathan went away to 'see to something', as he put it, and I helped Stella to get to bed. It wasn't long before we heard his well-known step on the stairs. There was a knock on the door, and when I opened it there he was, almost hidden behind an enormous bunch of chrysanthemums and goodness knows what else besides.

'A geranium in a pot!' cried Stella. 'How lovely! I've always wanted one, but I never seemed to have enough money left over to buy one. Oh, Jonathan – you shouldn't – you *shouldn't* have got me all these things. Why, you'll be absolutely broke!'

'Not a bit of it!' laughed Jonathan, tumbling bags of sweets pell-mell down on the counterpane. 'Didn't I tell you? I sold that little sketch of "Winter in the Cheviots" yesterday. Got quite a bit for it, too. What's the matter, Veronica? You look struck all of a heap.'

'I was just thinking of something,' I admitted. 'You know, while I was living with my cousins in Northumberland we had a Wayside Stall. I don't think I ever told you about it, did I, Jonathan?'

Jonathan shook his curly head.

'No. Out with it!'

'It's just that talking of paintings reminded me that we – Sebastian, Caroline, and I – put some of *my* choicest paintings on it. You remember the ones I used to do on the backs of your old canvases?'

He nodded.

'Do I not! You used to make me take my efforts off the frames and tack them on again the other way round!'

'Poor Jonathan! Well, as I say, I put them on our Wayside Stall to brighten it up a bit, and some highbrow people turned up and bought them. You see, they saw *your* things on the backs.'

Jonathan gave a great snort.

'Jumping Jehoshaphat! You don't mean to tell me, Veronica, that you sold that rubbish of mine to a lot of art dealers?'

'Not art dealers, Jonathan,' I corrected gently. 'They were a woman called Yvonne, and her brother. He had a little black beard – like yours.'

Jonathan groaned.

'Veronica! What have you done? That would be Yvonne and Claude Millhaven. They own most of the big art shops in these fashionable holiday resorts – like Cheltenham, Harrogate, Scarborough, and so forth. The Art Room, The Treasure Shop – you know the sort of thing! And you've sold them my – *my* canvases. I'm willing to bet that frightful daub, "Sunset on Skye", was one of them—' He groaned again.

'I'm afraid it was,' I admitted. 'I'm most awfully sorry, Jonathan.'

'Oh, well – I suppose it can't be helped,' said Jonathan philosophically.

'It was in aid of a very good cause,' I volunteered. 'The money was to hire me a pony to ride.'

'In that case,' said Jonathan grandly, 'you shall be forgiven. The affair shall be forgotten. Say no more!'

After this little incident we were all very happy. I sat on the end of Stella's bed, and Jonathan sat astride the one chair the room contained, and we all ate sweets and nuts and told funny stories. At about nine o'clock Jonathan said he'd have to go because he had a lot of work to do. I knew he meant housework; he always did it at night because of the light. I mean, he wanted the daylight for his painting, so he did his chores in the evening.

I said goodnight to Stella myself soon afterwards and went to my own room, for I was dead tired after my day's work. As I reached the door there was a roar from above my head, and, looking up, I beheld Jonathan's unruly black head looking over the banister rail. His teeth fairly shone in the dusk.

'Hey, Veronica! You might tell Stella that if I catch her up

33

and about tomorrow there'll be trouble! I'll be down with her breakfast about nine.'

'I'll tell her,' I shouted back.

While I was undressing that night I thought about Jonathan and what a puzzle he was. He didn't seem to be really poor. In fact, whenever any money was needed for anything, he'd always come forward. When Daddy had died, and I'd had to leave Mrs Crapper's house, they'd all made a collection for me as a goodbye present. I knew, from what Mrs Crapper said, that it was Jonathan who'd given the lion's share. Yet surely no one but a really poor person would live in Mrs Crapper's dingy apartment house. I'd once asked Jonathan why he went on living there, now that he was quite a well-known artist. He'd lit his old black pipe and puffed away at it very slowly for a long time before he answered.

'Well, Veronica,' he'd said at length. 'Perhaps it's because I want to look after you all – Mrs Crapper, dear soul, and you, Veronica, and Miriam before she went to the Windmill and got rich, and – and Stella. But, of course, you don't understand – you're too young.'

'Oh, no I'm not,' I assured him. 'I understand perfectly. I've often felt like that myself about dear Mrs Crapper – especially now that her eyes aren't what they were.'

'That's right; you've hit it!' said Jonathan, his eyes crinkling at the corners. 'So now you know why I stay on.'

But there were other things that puzzled me about Jonathan. He didn't seem to have any 'people' belonging to him, or if he had he never mentioned them. Yet he'd obviously been what Uncle John would call 'well brought up'. For instance, he'd always open the door for you, and let you go through first, and he'd stand up when you did. Also, I noticed that, although he worked with his old black pipe continually between his strong white teeth, he'd always stuff it into his pocket when he talked to us, or when he came and sat in Mrs Crapper's kitchen. Although his overalls were stained with paint and clay, his linen was spotless. He 'did' for himself, and although his

34

studio was littered with canvases, frames, palettes, brushes, and all the artist's paraphernalia, yet his bedroom and the little kitchen where he cooked his meals were spotlessly clean and tidy.

Yes, there was no doubt about it – Jonathan was a puzzle.

Chapter 4

We Celebrate

I DIDN'T see a great deal of Stella, apart from going to school
with her in the mornings and sharing the same dressing-room.
She was in the Senior class, of course; so all her lessons were
at different times to mine, and, besides that, she'd got several
parts in the Theatre Ballet, which is what is known to students
as the Second Company. We didn't often have lunch together
either, because she'd be rehearsing down at Sadler's Wells;
and most evenings she had performances, so I didn't even see
her then.

One day, towards the middle of term, just as I had arrived
home and was taking off my coat, I heard her voice on the
stairs.

'Veronica! – Jonathan! – I've the most wonderful news!
The most marvellous thing has happened!'

I dashed out on to the landing, and Jonathan appeared as if
by magic. Strangely enough, he always happened to be there
when Stella came home. Even Mrs Crapper came up from
below, wiping her hands on her apron.

'What is it, Stella?'

'I'm in!' said Stella, laughing and crying both at once. 'Yes,
it's true! I'm actually in the Company – the Second Company, of course.'

'Oh, Stella! How glorious!' I burst out. 'When did you get
to know?'

'This afternoon – at the three o'clock class. Miss Jackson,
the ballet mistress down at Sadler's Wells, you know, came in
and chose several of us. Belinda's one; but, of course, everyone
knew *she'd* be chosen; Mary and Jocelyn and me. We start on
Monday. Oh, isn't it glorious?'

'Glorious,' said Jonathan flatly.

'What's the matter?' said Stella, a pucker between her brows. 'Aren't you pleased?'

'Of course I'm pleased – if it's what you want,' Jonathan answered.

'Of *course* it's what I want.' Stella exclaimed. 'It's – why, it's my dream come true.'

'Well, now you'll have loads of money,' I said. 'You can have three-course lunches every day. You won't have to worry now; you're safe – permanently in the Company.'

A cloud passing over Stella's happy face and she gave a little sigh.

'There's nothing permanent in life,' she said soberly. 'Not in ballet, anyway. I might break my leg, or get fat, or anything. And that goes for the three-course lunches, too. I must think of my figure. My thighs are getting terribly big.'

'Let's not be gloomy now!' I exclaimed. 'Let's cast dull care aside and celebrate! Let's have fun! What show would you like to see most, Stella?'

Stella considered.

'I know it sounds funny and like a busman's holiday,' she said at length, 'but I'm simply longing to go to Covent Garden tomorrow night. It's Irma Foster in *Les Patineurs*, and they say it's her last performance. Ivan Stcherbakof is guest artist, and everyone says he's the most wonderful male dancer in the world. I might be able to get a free ticket from school. What about you, Veronica?'

I shook my head sadly.

'I had one last night for *Lac*, so I can't expect another this week. Anyway, Jonathan couldn't get one, so that's no use. How about going in the gallery slips? They're not too ruinous!'

'I've got an idea worth two of that,' Jonathan said quietly. 'How about doing it in style and going in a box?'

'A b-box?' Stella and I laughed both together in such awestruck voices that Jonathan laughed aloud.

'Are you joking, Jonathan?' I added. 'Why, a box at Covent Garden costs guineas and guineas!'

'Look – this is *my* treat,' Jonathan said firmly, 'so we won't discuss costs, if you don't mind. Didn't I tell you I sold a picture not so long ago?'

'Yes, but—'

'Don't argue, just leave it to me. We'll have a box for four and we'll take old Martha along with us, eh?'

'Oh, yes, that'll be lovely!' exclaimed Stella. 'I don't believe Mrs Crapper has ever been to what she calls "the bally". By the way, where *is* Mrs Crapper? She was here just a minute ago.'

'She went back to her kitchen when she heard your news, Stella,' said Jonathan. 'I don't think Martha realized how world-shattering it was! And, by the way,' he went on, 'we're going to see this performance as *ordinary theatre-goers*. Coffee in the first interval, ices in the second, and no going backstage.'

'All right,' Stella agreed. 'It'll be terribly queer, though.'

We didn't wear evening dress for our celebration. For once thing, I hadn't got a long frock yet, and for another we knew that Mrs Crapper would want to wear what she called 'me ciré lace'. This had been her wedding dress, but had been dyed black, being more useful that colour. Since Mrs Crapper's wedding day had been somewhere about 1919, the dress wasn't exactly what you might call the latest fashion. It was knee-length and had long flowing sleeves and a beige jabot that cascaded down the front like a waterfall. The waistline came somewhere about the knees. I can't imagine what the creation would have looked like on anybody else, but it certainly suited Mrs Crapper as no other dress would have done. On top of the ciré lace she wore 'me fur coat', which was a mat-like garment smelling of mothballs, and on top of the lot went a pudding-basin hat with a bunch of glass grapes at one side which rattled when she moved. When she was dressed in her best,

Mrs Crapper adopted a slightly aloof manner to go with her finery, except when excitement overcame her, and she forgot!

When we had settled ourselves in our box we scanned the programme eagerly to see who were dancing the principal roles.

'*Les Patineurs*,' read out Stella. 'The classical *pas-de-deux*, Foster and Linsk; *pas-seul*, Ivan Stcherbakof; that's the Exhibition Skater in blue,' she added for Jonathan's benefit. '*Spectre de la Rose*, with Stcherbakof and Beryl Grey. *The Rake's Progress*, with Gordon Hamilton as 'The Rake', and – let me see, oh, yes, Linsk as the Dancing Master. I love the Dancing Master, don't you?'

'I've never seen the ballet,' I confessed.

It was lovely watching the ballet from the front and being looked after. Jonathan produced a box of chocolates from his overcoat pocket, and we ordered ices and coffee as he had promised. As for Mrs Crapper – she sat with her eyes glued to the stage, watching the skating couples. Every few minutes she'd say in an awestruck voice: 'Ee, but it's lovely! All them folk skating to the manner born!' When the solitary Skater in Blue appeared, she was spellbound.

'There now! You wouldn't believe it, would you? My! but he's a grand skater, and no mistake! Good enough for an exhibition, I shouldn't wonder. He oughta be in them Ice Folies, he should that! I'm told they're wonderful, and very well paid.'

It wasn't a bit of good trying to explain to Mrs Crapper that Ivan Stcherbakof was a *dancer*, and not a skater at all; that he was world famous, and that he wouldn't be in the least bit flattered by being told he ought to be in the Ice Folies, however marvellous or well paid they might be.

'Gosh! Isn't he wonderful?' whispered Stella as we watched him breathlessly. 'He's even better than they say. He's electrified the whole house!' Indeed, there wasn't a sound from that great audience – not a cough or the rustle of a programme – so thrilled was it by the brilliant personality of the young Russian dancer.

Ivan Stcherbakof: the Exhibition Skater in Blue

'They say he has the best elevation since Nijinski,' whispered Stella. 'I can quite believe it, can't you? When he jumps, it's just a like a bird flying!'

The young man in blue was followed by a skating couple in white – the classical *pas-de-deux*.

'Irma Foster,' said Stella. 'You haven't seen her before, have you, Veronica? She doesn't often appear now. She's thirty-eight, you know, and that's old for a dancer.'

Irma Foster was very beautiful. If she lacked brilliance on account of her age, she certainly made up for it with other things. Her dancing was aristocratic in the extreme, and her line was so pure she made you think of fields of virgin snow and frosted fir branches; of a calm frozen lake with the moonlight shining down upon it out of the northern sky.

Then the lovely slow music of the classical *pas-de-deux* changed to the urgent, compelling melody for the girls in brown and blue, and then two others in maroon and white. The latter had evidently not learned to skate very well, for they kept slipping! At last some young men arrived on the scene to help them, and gallantly pulled them across the frozen pool. The ballet now worked up to an exciting finish, the whole Company whirling round the stage in various figures. At last they all skated away, leaving the Exhibition Skater turning his endless *fouettés* on the icy pool. The light faded, the snow began to fall, but still he turned effortlessly. As the curtain fell he was still spinning, and you felt that he would go on spinning for ever.

'Wonderful ballet!' Stella said with a sigh of happiness. 'I can't count the number of times I've seen it, but I like it better each time.'

'I saw it once, ages ago,' I said, 'but it wasn't nearly as good as it was tonight. That young man – Ivan Stcherbakof – is a marvellous dancer, and Irma Foster is lovely too.'

The lights went on and the coffee arrived, brought by a pert usherette who stared at Jonathan in open admiration. Mrs Crapper produced a pair of ancient opera-glasses out of her handbag, and we amused ourselves by getting close-ups of the people in the auditorium.

'Look!' said Stella. 'You see that little girl in the fifth row of the stalls – the one with the bright red-gold hair and the brown velvet dress with the lace collar? That's Mariella Foster, Irma Foster's only daughter. They say she's training to be a dancer herself. I wonder if she'll be any good at it?'

'Shouldn't think so,' put in Jonathan. 'The talent has probably culminated in the mother, and the kid will be something altogether different, I expect – like a doctor or a mathematician.'

'Do you see the man she's with? That's Oscar Deveraux, her father. He's a famous critic, but in spite of that he's always known as "Irma Foster's husband", poor little man!'

'Why is the kid's name Foster, when her father's name is Deveraux?' I asked.

'Well, Irma Foster made her name long before she met Oscar Deveraux,' explained Stella. 'So she still dances under her maiden name, though really she's Mrs Oscar Deveraux. The kid's known by her mother's name too – for dancing purposes. I expect she's hoping for a bit of reflected glory! ... Well, it's *Spectre de la Rose* next. I wonder what Stcherbakof will be like as the Spirit of the Rose? It's a question not only of technique, but "feeling", if you know what I mean.'

'Perhaps he'll be even better than he was in *Les Patineurs*,' I answered. 'I wonder if he'll give us some idea of what Nijinski was like. I wonder—'

But the packed auditorium was destined never to see the brilliant Russian's interpretation of the famous role. We had just given back our empty coffee cups to the attendant, and were watching the members of the orchestra filing back into their pit, when suddenly Stella gripped my arm.

'Look!' she whispered. 'Something's happened! There's going to be an announcement. That's the stage manager, and he's going to speak.'

There was a short roll of drums, and the noise in the

auditorium died down as if by magic. It was so quiet that you could hear the clink of cups and glasses, and the hum of voices from the crush-bar. Then these sounds died away, too, as the news spread that an announcement was being made.

'Lords, ladies, and gentlemen,' said the manager. 'I very much regret to have to tell you that Monsieur Ivan Stcherbakof has had a slight accident. His place in *Le Spectre de la Rose* will be taken by Mr Josef Linsk.'

There was an audible sigh from the audience. One or two people in the gallery, who were Linsk fans, clapped feebly, but were drowned by the disapproving 'sh' of their neighbours of better taste. The feeling of the house was undoubtedly that of disappointment. Of course, Linsk was a brilliant dancer, but he was a member of the Company; they could see him any time. Moreover, they had come especially to see the world-famous Russian, and, after his brilliant exhibition in *Les Patineurs*, they were unable to hide their disappointment at not seeing him dance again. Yes, Ivan Stcherbakof had indeed captured the hearts and fired the imagination of the large audience.

'I can't believe it!' said Stella, when the manager had disappeared behind the curtain. 'I simply *can't* believe it! Why, only a minute ago he was turning those *fouettés* in the middle of the stage. What can have happened?'

'He must have tripped over something,' I said. 'Or fallen down some stairs.'

'Or perhaps bumped into someone,' Jonathan put in. 'I was once at a performance of *Coppélia* in which there was a proper chapter of accidents. Moira Shearer had a collision with Veronica Vale, and poor Veronica put her kneecap out, and had to sit on the stage with it out until the curtain went down. Things like that are always happening to ballet dancers.'

We both stared at Jonathan.

'I didn't know you knew anything about ballet, Jonathan,' said Stella. 'I always thought you despised it.'

'On the contrary – I love it,' Jonathan said. 'I've yet to meet an artist who doesn't.'

'Well, I never knew that!' Stella said in amazement.

Jonathan smiled down at her.

'I don't think you really know an awful lot about me, Stella,' he said.

'Whatever do you mean?' Stella said indignantly. 'Why, I've known you ever since I was a kid.'

'Perhaps that's why,' Jonathan said enigmatically.

'I wish you'd stop talking in riddles,' Stella said crossly. 'If I don't know everything there is to know about you, I should like to know who does?'

'Sh!' said Jonathan warningly. 'The curtain's going up!'

The rest of the performance was a sad come-down after the beginning. Nothing is so sensitive to atmosphere as a theatre audience, and we all felt that something awful had happened, and that the dancers were merely living up to the old adage: 'The show must go on.' They were dancing with their feet, all right, but their hearts weren't in it.

As we came out into the frosty night Stella plucked Jonathan by the sleeve.

'I simply must fly round to the stage door and see what's happened,' she said. 'I shan't be long. Wait for me here.'

In a very few minutes she was back again.

'Oh, it's awful!' she said, with a sob in her voice. 'Someone had left a tube of greasepaint lying on the stairs going up to the dressing-rooms, and he slipped on it, and fell right down to the bottom. All those awful stone stairs! He's hurt his knee, and they think it's pretty bad – you can tell by the way they talk. They've taken him to the hospital straight away for an X-ray. Oh, Jonathan – Veronica – isn't it awful! Poor, poor man!'

As we walked home under the frosty sky I thought of the young Russian dancer, struck down at the height of his fame, and in my imagination I still saw him turning his effortless *fouettés* on the frozen pool, with the snowflakes falling all around him like tears.

Chapter 5

A Pair of Tights

THE news was all over the school when I got there next morning. Tongues wagged a hundred to the dozen.

'Ivan Stcherbakof ... yes, on the stone staircase going up to the dressing-rooms ... never dance again, they say ... oh, you never can tell; remember Bettini? Everyone said ... slipped on a tube of greasepaint. Golly! How awful for the person who dropped it! Imagine going down in history as the owner of the greasepaint Stcherbakof slipped on! ... Marcia was there when they carried him out on the stretcher; she says he looked like Death. Tell us what he looked like, Marcia ... Did you hear the house groan when they gave it out? Gosh! Josef would be mad! Not used to playing second-fiddle ... conceited? I should just say so! ... What? You don't think he is? But of course you *wouldn't* – I forgot you had a crush on Josef ... Hullo, Veronica! Heard the news?'

'Yes, I was in the theatre when it happened – in the audience,' I answered. 'Do you think it's serious?'

'Oh, yes – fatal, I should say,' Belinda said cheerfully, pulling up her tights. 'He's probably broken his back.'

'Oh, *no*!' I said with a gasp of horror. 'It's only his knee. They said so, didn't they, Stella?'

Stella nodded. She'd come with me as usual. As she didn't start in the Company until Monday, she had to attend classes until then.

'Yes, Mr Rogers said it was a slight accident when he gave it out.'

Belinda shrugged her shoulders.

'Oh, you can't go by *that*,' she declared. 'They always make light of an accident that happens to anyone famous. It's like royalty – if they gave it out on the radio that the Queen has got a slight cold, you can bet your life she's pretty bad. By the way, I expect you've all heard I'm to go into the Company on Monday. Anyone like a pair of old tights?' She threw the tights into the middle of the floor, whereupon they became the centre of what looked like a rugger scrum.

'He who fights gets tights!' she yelled, dancing about on her toes like a referee at a boxing match. 'Odds on Lily! She's got a hard head!'

Lily did indeed emerge victorious, if dishevelled, the tights clutched firmly under one arm.

'I shall have to change my name,' went on Belinda. 'It's essential now I'm really in the Company.'

'Your name?' echoed Lily, her mind obviously still on the tights.

'Yes, my daydreamer. My *name*. N-A-M-E. Can't go on the stage as Belinda Stout, now can I? Think of it in the repertoire of *The Sleeping Beauty*: "Fonteyn and Soames, with Stout as the Lilac Fairy! . . . The classic role of the Queen of the Wilis in the romantic ballet, *Giselle*, was danced most gracefully by Stout . . .'

'You don't dance the Queen of the Wilis *gracefully*,' I put in firmly. 'You dance it coldly and inhumanly.'

'You *would* think of that, Veronica Weston,' said Belinda, not sounding too pleased at being corrected. 'Anyway, you don't dance it *stoutly*. I shall change my name to Beaucaire. Belinda Beaucaire,' she repeated dreamily. 'Goes well, doesn't it?'

'But you aren't French,' objected Sara.

'No more is Margot Fonteyn – or de Valois herself, for that matter. Yes, I'm quite determined – I shall be Belinda Beaucaire.'

She began to turn *déboulées* across the dressing-room, almost colliding with someone coming in at the door.

'Hullo, June! What's up?' she exclaimed, finishing off the

*déboulée*s with a treble *pirouette*. 'You look struck all of a heap!'

'Do I?' laughed June. 'That's always the effect Madame has upon me!'

It was our turn to look struck all of a heap, as Belinda put it.

'Madame? ... Madame ...' The name had the effect of an electric shock upon the lazy dressing-room.

'Yes – Madame the Director, herself. I suppose you *have* heard of her?' said June sarcastically. As if anyone hadn't! 'Well, she's on her way here. I heard old Willan talking to her on the telephone – the office door was open, so it wasn't like eavesdropping. She's coming to take the Junior class – Madame, I mean.'

The effect of this speech was a series of sounds raging from excited squeals to yelps and groans.

'Gosh, how awful! My tights ...' This was Lily.

'Madame! How wonderful!' This Belinda. 'How I wish I was still of the Juniors for just this one morning! Wouldn't I enjoy myself!'

'Madame herself!' I murmured. At last I'd really see her – be taught by her. To be taught by Madame – wonderful, legendary Madame – seemed to me to be the height of bliss. At the back of my mind I could hear a babel of voices. The dressing-room had got over the shock and was becoming really excited.

'Do you think this hairband will dry in time if I put it on the radiator?' ... 'You'd better unplait your hair, Sara – she likes it done on top in a scarf. Oh, I know yours stays up as if it was glued, but remember the fuss there was when Jacqueline's came down last time!' ... 'Has anybody got a darning needle and a bit of cotton? These tights.' ... 'Here you are, darling! I know the thread's green, but it'll be better than nothing.' ... 'Thanks awfully, Mary. Now if I only had a bit of elastic for my trunks.' ... 'Anyone got a spot of elastic for Delia's trunks? *I* know! I'll give you the bit off my hat. It'll

47

be tight, but you can put up with it for just this morning. What it is to have brains!' ... 'Golly! Look at Veronica! She's in a brown study! Wake up, Veronica! You'd better buck up and change or you'll be late.'

The words reached my subconscious mind. I gave myself a shake and looked round for my case. It lay open on the bench near the window.

'Gosh! Yes – I must change like a flash! My tights—' I rummaged in my case for them, but they weren't there.

'Have any of you seen my tights?' I yelled in a panic.

'This seems to be a general refrain!' drawled Marcia Rutherford. 'Don't say you've lost *your* tights, too, Veronica Weston? I thought you never lost *anything*.'

I hardly heard her. I was searching frantically in every nook and cranny of the dressing-room – under the benches, on the table littered with other people's belongings, behind the radiators, everywhere.

'You've probably left them at home,' Sara said, joining in the search. 'I'm always doing things like that. Last week it was my hairpins, and I had to fasten my hair up with nails and string! Think back – when did you have them last?'

'This morning,' I answered, crawling round on my hands and knees. 'I *know* I put them in my case because I had to carry my sandwiches separately; they wouldn't go in as well.'

'Sure it wasn't yesterday?' put in June.

'No, it wasn't; it was today,' I said firmly.

'Have you tried the lost-property office?' said Taiis helpfully.

'Gosh, no!' I dashed away to the little office, opening off the entrance hall, where all the things we lost, or were found lying about on the floor, were impounded. But there were no pink tights with 'Veronica Weston' on them. In fact, there were no tights at all, or I might have persuaded Elizabeth, the assistant secretary, to let me borrow them for just this one class.

When I got back to the dressing-room I found it empty. The Juniors had gone off to the Baylis Hall to be ready for

Madame; the Seniors to their Character class with Serge.

I sat down on a bench by the door, my heart filled with despair. What was I to do? Go into class without tights? Unthinkable! I'd be sent out in disgrace on the spot. Nobody – nobody ever attended a ballet class without tights – let alone Madame's class.

A tear stole down my nose. I'd waited so long for this chance – the chance to shine in Madame's eyes – and now, it seemed, it was going to be denied me. I wasn't even going to *see* Madame, let alone be taught by her. As I sat there, my thoughts flew to the Baylis Hall where the others were all enjoying this honour. I heard in my imagination the tinkle of the piano, Madame's voice crisply giving orders, addressing Gilbert, singling me out ... 'What is the name of the dark child in the back row, Mr Delahaye? Yes, the second from the end? I like her. She has a good "line". Very promising ... Come farther forward, dear...'

The telephone ringing in the Director's office broke in upon my daydream. Oh, well – crying about it didn't help. I'd better wash my face, and forget about it.

I went over to the mirror and looked at myself critically. Yes, I certainly was in a bit of a mess. My dark eyes had smudges round them where I'd rubbed them, my hair was untidy, my nose red. I walked round the dressing-room, collecting up my belongings. Although I was usually fairly tidy, I'd been in such a frantic state about the disappearance of my tights that I'd scattered my things all over the place. My towel was on the floor, and my soap had skidded across the table and shot underneath one of the radiators. As I poked it out I nearly upset a bowl of dirty water deposited on the floor by Mrs Wopping, the charwoman, when she'd been cleaning the windows. Mrs Wopping was anything but a tidy soul, and the school was strewn with her wash-leathers, dusters, floorcloths, and all the other insignia of her calling. Whenever Mrs Wopping was mildly reproved by the authorities for her untidy ways, she replied with dignity: 'I does me work in me own

49

way, and if it ain't satisfactory, there's a remedy.' She never
went so far as to give the remedy a name, but spent the rest of
the day muttering ominously: 'take it or leave it ... warning
... notice given ... folk as oughta mind their own business.'
Then the whole affair would blow over, and for a few days
tidiness would reign. But before very long, back would come
the dusters and the floorcloths, and all would be as before. In
disgust I poked at the dirty cloth that raised its head in Mrs
Wopping's inky water like an inquiring seal, or a volcanic
island in the midst of the ocean. Then I bent closer. Somehow
it didn't look like a floorcloth. It looked familiar – like – like –
yes, it *was*! It was my tights!

I fished the filthy object out of the water and wrung it out.
Yes, there was no doubt about it. My tears began to flow
afresh. It was so awful to realize that my tights had been there
all the time, right under my very nose, and it wasn't much of a
consolation to know that they wouldn't have been the least use
to me if I *had* found them. For a long time I stood there,
wondering how the dreadful thing had happened. I was still
puzzling my brain when the door opened and Sara dashed
in.

'It's all right, Veronica!' she panted. 'You needn't cry. I
dashed down to tell you – said I wanted to change into my
point shoes – Madame didn't turn up after all.'

'What? *What* did you say?'

'No – she rang up and said that someone had come to see
her just as she was setting out to come here – someone most
awfully important, so she couldn't come after all. The Director sent up a message. Didn't you hear the phone? Oh, but of
course you wouldn't know it had anything to do with Madame.
And anyway, I don't expect you even *heard* it – you'd be
thinking of us in the Baylis Hall being taught by Madame, I
shouldn't wonder. You're an awful dreamer, you know,
Veronica!'

'I know I am,' I laughed. 'And you're quite right. I've been
sitting here having the most wonderful class with Madame –

even if it *was* all in my imagination. I expect when I *do* have a class with her, it won't be a bit like that!'

'No – I expect it won't,' agreed Sara. 'By the way, what are you holding that dirty old thing for? I suppose it's old Wopping's floorcloth?'

'You suppose wrong!' I answered. 'This dirty old thing' – I held aloft the dripping black object – 'this is my tights.'

Sara stopped in the middle of tying on her point shoes, and her eyes flew wide.

'Your *tights*? But how on earth did they get in there?'

'That's exactly what I was asking myself when you came in,' I answered. 'I simply can't *think*. I'm pretty sure old Wopping—'

'It's not old Wopping's doing,' declared Sara, cutting me short. 'She would never do a thing like that. Of course, I can't *prove* anything, but I've a shrewd idea I know who it was.'

'You mean?'

'I mean Marcia,' said Sara. 'You see, I've just remembered something. Last term we had a class with Miss Jackson from the Theatre Ballet – an important class. Well, Delia's tights disappeared. We couldn't find them *anywhere*. Just at the last moment, when everyone had gone into class and poor Delia was in despair, who should walk in but Marcia and offer to lend her a spare pair. Delia put them on, and they happened to be fishnet ones, which aren't allowed – goodness knows why, but they aren't. Well, Delia didn't know about the rule because she was new, and she got sent out of the room in disgrace.'

'How awful!' I said in horror. 'I seem to have got off lightly. I'd have died if I'd been poor Delia and got sent out of class.'

'Well, if I don't stop gossiping, *I* shall be sent out of Gilbert's class!' Sara laughed. 'I'm supposed to be putting on my point shoes, and I've been down here a quarter of an hour already. So long, Veronica! See you after class!'

51

With this she was gone, and I was alone once more. But this time I didn't care. I hadn't missed anything after all. I was so relieved that I turned *déboulées* all·down the dressing-room, finishing with a treble *pirouette* as much like Belinda's as possible. My class with Madame was yet to come!

Chapter 6

The Swimming Baths

AFTER the affair of the tights, I kept as far away from Marcia Rutherford as I could, but sometimes it was impossible. The weather was warm for November – at least, it seemed warm to me in comparison with Northumberland, where I had lived all last year. Most of the others thought it was chilly, though, and when I suggested going to the swimming baths before afternoon school, they shivered.

'The swimming baths?' echoed Sara. 'Ugh! Not for me! I'm not one of your Spartan people! I couldn't go, in any case, because I have an Advanced Mime class from two to three. What on earth do you want to go swimming in November for, Veronica? It's not civilized!'

'When I lived with my cousins, Fiona and Caroline, we used to go swimming in the lake in the grounds,' I explained. 'And once Sebastian broke the ice on it. Sebastion was Fiona and Caroline's cousin, and he was an awfully good swimmer. Well, when I passed by the baths today, I saw a placard of a swimming gala, and that made me think of the lake at Bracken Hall, and that made me want to go swimming. I feel I simply *must* go swimming today, or bust!'

'Well, don't bust!' laughed Sara. 'Too messy! I expect June will go with you. She's another of the Spartan kind.'

But June wasn't keen either.

'Matter of fact,' she said apologetically, 'I've got a bit of a sore throat. Mother would take a fit if I went swimming. Marcia and Kay usually go on Fridays, though. Are you going to the baths today, Kay?'

Kay said she was, and Marcia too. I wasn't a bit keen on their company – especially Marcia's – but I could hardly say so, because Kay really wasn't a bad sort of girl. Her only crime was that she was a friend of Marcia's.

'Oh, all right – I may see you there,' I said, rather unenthusiastically.

'By the way, Veronica,' put in Sara. 'You won't be late for afternoon class, with you? It's the audition for the Youth Festival, remember.'

'The Youth Festival?' I repeated, coming back into the dressing-room. 'I've never heard of it.'

'Oh, I forgot,' said Sara. 'You'd gone home yesterday when Miss Willan came into the dressing-room and told us about it. It's not terribly important, but it would be a first part for you.'

I stared at her, aghast. Not terribly important! My very first part!

'Tell me all about it,' I urged, putting my towel and bathing costume down on the centre table. 'It sounds thrilling!'

'Well, it's to be in Finsbury Park,' explained Sara, 'and we're to do the ballet part – demonstrate the different kinds of dancing, and so on. Miss Jackson, from the Theatre Ballet, is coming to class this afternoon to choose people for it. She's in charge of the dancing part of the Youth Festival.'

'I'll be there,' I assured her. 'Trust me not to be late for an audition! Gosh! What a good thing you told me about it, Sara!'

'Well, you'd have been there in any case,' laughed Sara. 'You're never late for any of the classes, Veronica – not even Eurhythmics!'

It was lovely at the swimming baths. The water felt beautifully warm – a lot warmer than it does in the summertime when the air outside is hot. I wondered why more people didn't go swimming in the winter.

Marcia and Kay had cubicles next to mine, but fortunately neither of them could swim well, so, once I was in the water, I didn't see much of them. I spent most of my time in the deep end, diving off the high springboard.

As I swam leisurely towards the steps to have yet another dive, Marcia came running towards me along the edge.

'Oh, Veronica,' she shouted. 'I'm going out now. Would you mind if I did my hair in your cubicle? The mirror in mine is cracked right across.'

'All right,' I yelled back – the baths were anything but a quiet place. 'You can have five minutes – no more. I'm coming out then – mustn't be late for class.'

When I hauled myself, dripping, on to the edge of the bath at the end of the five minutes, and pattered back to my cubicle, Marcia had already gone, leaving stray hairs all over the little corner shelf, and a cloud of heavily scented face powder on my mirror. I wiped it off with my hankie, and scanned my hair anxiously. Oh, well, I thought, if it *was* rather wet, it would be all the tidier for the audition.

As I dressed I nibbled one of Mrs Crapper's sandwiches that she'd given me that morning to eat with my mid-morning milk. Then, when I'd pulled on my frock, I glanced at my wristwatch, where it lay on the shelf beside my kirbygrips, just to make sure I'd got plenty of time.

It wasn't as late as I'd thought – only half-past two. As my class wasn't till three-thirty, I had loads of time.

'What about a coffee at the snack bar round the corner,' suggested Marcia, joining me on the steps outside.

'Oh, I don't think I'd better,' I said doubtfully. 'There's my class, you see—'

'Well, of course don't let me influence you,' said Marcia, 'but I'd say you really *ought* to have something hot before your class. If you go dancing with nothing to eat after your swim, you may collapse or something during the audition – you never know!'

'Oh, I wouldn't do that!' I laughed. 'Anyway, I've already had one of Martha's sandwiches – and they're not dainty, afternoon-tea sort of sandwiches, I can tell you!'

'OK. Don't say I didn't warn you,' declared Marcia.

Suddenly I turned back and walked along with her.

'Perhaps you're right,' I said. 'I think I will have a coffee after all. By the way, where's Kay?'

'Oh, she had to dash off – she'd got some shopping to do for her mother. Proper slave driver is Kay's mother! It's all right, Veronica – you've loads of time,' she added, seeing my eyes on my watch. 'It's only just twenty-five to three.'

Hastily I swallowed a cup of hot coffee and ate a bun. After this I stood up firmly.

'I really must go now, Marcia. I've simply got to find a shop that sells hairnets. If I'd only known this morning that there was an audition today I'd have got it then.'

'Gosh! What a fuss about a stupid little audition!' sneered Marcia. 'Anyone would think it was to get into the Company!'

'Well, it may seem unimportant to you,' I retorted, 'you've had lots of small parts, and you're dancing with the Second Company now – but it's very important to me. Goodbye, Marcia.'

'S'long, Veronica,' said Marcia, adding sarcastically: 'I do hope you're not late for the audition.'

I tried several shops before I found one that sold hairnets – not the fine ones you use during the daytime, but the strong coarse ones. It had to be dark, too, so that it wouldn't look like a sleeping-cap. I got it at last, however, and dashed into the Underground.

I looked at my wrist-watch again. Just after three. It was only ten minutes in the Underground to Baron's Court, so I really had plenty of time. All the same, I began to wish I hadn't had the coffee after all. I wasn't going to have as much time to get ready as I liked – not for such an important thing as an audition! Thank goodness, I thought, the Underground wasn't like a bus – at least you couldn't be held up by a traffic-block!

As I dashed out of Baron's Court station and hurried round the square to Colet Gardens, I glanced up at the clock of St Paul's School. I just couldn't believe my eyes – it said ten minutes to *four*!

'No,' I said aloud. 'It can't be! It's impossible! Why, it was only just after three when I left the coffee bar.'

I looked down at my wristwatch and held it to my ear. Yes, it was wound up all right, and it said a quarter past three. Clearly something must be wrong with St Paul's clock.

But, with a sinking heart, I knew that it wasn't St Paul's clock that was wrong – it was my watch. I remembered Marcia doing her hair in my cubicle, putting her comb on my shelf, cheek by jowl with my watch, and I knew what had happened as clearly as if I had seen it. She had altered the hands of my watch and put it half an hour slow. But, of course, I couldn't *prove* it. It was all what you might call circumstantial evidence. With a lump in my throat, I heard the tinkle of the piano in the Baylis Hall, and knew that in there was the great Miss Jackson, choosing out all the lucky people who were to be in the Youth Festival. And I – I was left out.

I sat down on a bench in the dressing-room, and wept. If I had only known what Fate had in store for me up her sleeve, I'd have laughed and shouted for glee. Yes, I'd have chuckled to think that Marcia Rutherford, of all people, had done me a good turn instead of a bad one. If it hadn't been for Marcia Rutherford, I'd have been in the Youth Festival, and then—

But all this was in the far-distant future. I must keep to the present, and, as I said before, I was very miserable on that November afternoon as I sat alone in the deserted dressing-room.

Chapter 7

A Visit to the Zoo

MARCIA seemed determined to act the role of my bad angel. One morning, near the end of term, she turned to me and announced in a triumphant tone of voice:

'Oh, by the way, Veronica, you'll have to be getting another partner for Character. Toni's been taken into the Company – the Second Company down at the Wells, I mean, of course.'

I said nothing, but my heart was full of dismay. Toni had been my mainstay in the Character class. No one knew what a help he'd been to me; I would miss him terribly. Still, I was glad he was getting his chance.

Meanwhile, the whole dressing-room was agog.

'Toni Rossini?' echoed June in astonishment. 'Why, he hasn't been in the school for more than a couple of terms. Of course he's good – there's no denying it. Still—'

'He worked with George Lejeune for ages,' Belinda put in. 'He was fully trained before ever he came to the Wells. Besides, he's an up-and-coming choreographer – no end of an asset to a company these days. Remember that ballet he made up for the RAD Production Club – *The Sailor's Wife*? Well, they're going to do it down at Sadler's Wells.'

'Golly! Are they really,' Sara said in an awestruck voice. 'He *must* be marvellous. Good old Toni! I always said he'd get on.'

'He'll probably fizzle out.' Marcia said with a shrug. 'Those brilliant sort generally do.' She flashed a look of hatred at the unconscious Belinda, who was now using the edge of the dressing-room table for *pas-de-deux* practice. 'It's fatal to be too good at the beginning.'

'*You* ought to be OK, then, Marcia,' Delia put in rather

58

nastily, I have to admit; but, then, I consider that Marcia had asked for it.

'Are you ready, Veronica?' said Taiis from the door. 'It is five minutes to three.'

'Just coming,' I answered, buttoning the straps of my Character shoes. 'Don't wait for me.'

I can't say that I enjoyed the Character class as much as usual that day. All the time I executed the gay, peasant steps, I was thinking to myself: 'This is the last time I shall dance with Toni. The last time ... the very last time.'

At the end of the class we said goodbye solemnly.

'The very best of luck, Toni,' I said. 'And – and thank you for being so decent to me.'

I turned away so that he shouldn't see there were tears in my eyes. But it was too late – he had already seen.

'Why, Veronique!' he exclaimed. 'What, then, is the matter? You are crying?'

'It's n-nothing,' I gulped. 'It's only that I may n-never see you again.'

Toni laughed.

'Not see me again? But, of course, you will see me again – of course, of course! Why not?'

'I may n-never get into the Company,' I said with a catch in my breath. 'S-sometimes when I see B-Belinda turning *pirouettes* so wonderfully, I feel I shall never, never be able to do them like that.'

'Belinda?' repeated Toni. 'Ah, she is the girl with the hair of red. She is good – that is true. She is brilliant – yes. But you are good, too, Veronique. You will, perhaps, be better than this Belinda one day, when you acquire the technique. You have more of the soul in your training.'

'It's sweet of you to say so, Toni,' I said through my tears. 'And now – goodbye again, Toni.'

'One moment, Veronique,' Toni said, putting a hand on my arm. 'Why should we not have a, what you call him – a little celebration? Why should we not go somewhere – anywhere you wish – and drink to my good fortune and to your future, in the squash of a lemon?'

I burst out laughing at his funny English.

'Oh, that would be *lovely*!' I exclaimed. 'There's practically nothing I like quite so much as the squash of a lemon!'

'Where, then, shall we drink it?' urged Toni. 'Where most would you like to go, Veronique?'

'The Zoo,' I said promptly. 'I've got a pet monkey in the Zoo. I call him Jacko, and I want to say goodbye to him.'

'Goodbye?' echoed Toni, with rasied eyebrows. 'You go away?'

'Oh, don't be alarmed!' I laughed. 'I'm not going away for good or anything – only for the holidays. Exactly a week tomorrow I shall be on my way to Northumberland.'

'Ah, your home, he is in the north of England, then?' said Toni.

'Well, you see, I've sort of got two homes,' I told him. 'Before Daddy died, we lived in London. But afterwards, I went to live with my cousins in Northumberland. I didn't like it much at first – it was all so different, but now – well, sometimes I get most frightfully homesick for the moors and the fir wood and Arabesque, my pony. I think it's partly because my mother was North Country.'

'Yes, I expect that is so,' Toni answered gravely. 'I am happy that you have somewhere joyful to go in the holidays. And now – about this celebration of ours. Will the morning of Sunday be convenient for you?'

'Oh, but you can't go to the Zoo on Sunday morning!' I objected.

'Oh, yes, you can – if you have got a member's card,' Toni assured me. 'Both my father and I have one.'

'Your father?' I said. 'I didn't know you had a father. At least, I mean, I didn't know he was in London.'

'Oh, yes,' said Toni. 'He is at the Italian Embassy. He is

very fond of animals, my father, and so we go most of the mornings of Sunday and look at the queer creatures in the Zoo. We like the snakes especially.'

'Snakes? Ugh!' I said with a shudder. 'I think snakes are ghastly!'

'Ghastly, but fascinating,' said Toni with a smile. 'Well, our celebration, he is then settled. It is to be the Zoo on the morning of Sunday. Where shall we meet?'

'Oh, I'll be at the main gates at eleven o'clock,' I answered, 'if you're quite sure you want to go with me.'

'Quite sure, Veronique,' Toni assured me gravely.

It was a lovely day on Sunday, not a bit like November, and even the thought that I was losing my helpful dancing partner couldn't depress me. The Zoo was beautifully quiet and select, and we were able to feed the animals without crowds of people breathing down our necks. Even the panda came out and looked at us sleepily, as if he knew we were distinguished Sunday members!

We made our way slowly to the cages where those queer-looking members of the monkey tribe, the mandrills, are kept. My little monkey, Jacko, was in a cage alongside, and we fed him with nuts and liquorice all-sorts, which he loves. In the next cage was a most evil-looking baboon, all-over multi-coloured stripes and spots that made him appear as if he'd got some awful disease. I think he must have got out of bed on the wrong side that morning, for he wasn't at all friendly. Whenever we tried to give him something to eat he sprang at us, rattling the bars and shaking the whole cage in his fury. So we left him and spent most of our time feeding Jacko.

Someone had given Jacko an ancient bus conductor's peaked cap, and he was having the time of his life with it, putting it on at the most absurd and rakish angles and causing roars of laughter among the onlookers by lifting it politely whenever an especially well-dressed lady paused in front of his cage. I expect he'd noticed visitors doing this and had stored the idea away in his clever little brain, to trot out on some future occasion. He certainly liked to be the centre of attraction, did Jacko, and very soon he was in his element with quite a crowd in front of his cage.

It was after we'd been there some time that I noticed two particularly unprepossessing schoolboys lounging among the spectators. One of them, whose name appeared to be Hamish, had bright red hair, blue eyes, and a wide, thick-lipped mouth. He looked about fifteen, but might have been older because, between his thick lips, dangled a cigarette. He puffed away at it for a time, staring at Jacko with his little blue eyes; then, to my horror, he quietly passed the lighted cigarette through the bars to the little monkey, and stood back in the crowd. None of the onlookers seemed to realize what had happened except me, and I expect that was because I always regarded Jacko as my own little monkey.

I stood in front of the cage in an agony of indecision, hoping that Jacko would drop the cigarette on the floor when he saw it was lit. But he didn't; instead he put it straight into his mouth.

After this there was pandemonium. Poor Jacko spat out the cigarette, and fled gibbering to the roof of the cage, where he clung, huddled against the wall, whimpering and moaning, and blinking down at us piteously with his sad brown eyes. Real tears ran down his wrinkled cheeks, and all the time he stroked his face with his little paws, as if trying to take away the pain. You could almost see him telling the people all about the wicked boy who had played him such a mean trick.

I turned round to look for the boy, rage in my heart. Yes, there he was, hovering at the back of the crowd, with a hateful grin on his silly face.

'That's the boy who did it!' I yelled to the astonished people, and I pointed to the red-haired Hamish. 'That's the boy – the one with the beastly red hair! He gave Jacko, my darling monkey, a lighted cigarette. How dare he! How dare he!'

I sprang at Hamish, the crowd parting, like the Red Sea did before the Israelites, to let me through.

Vaguely I heard Toni's voice behind me.

'One moment, Veronique – allow me, please—'

But I was past taking any notice of Toni, or anyone else. Hamish was rapidly making his escape, and I wasn't going to allow that – not if I knew it!

We crashed down the paths, the boy dodging this way and that, with me close on his heels. People turned round to stare at us – I think they imagined we were playing Hide and Seek, or Tag, and by their disapproving expressions I could see that they were going to complain about us to the management – playing such rowdy games on a Sunday morning of all days! But I didn't care. I was determined to bring my enemy to justice.

We crashed past an enclosure full of queer, long-necked birds which fled in terror at our approach. Then up we dashed into the galleries above the Bear Pit, and down again, Hamish drawing ahead a little but not very much.

Suddenly the Snake House loomed up in front of me. I shot round the corner of it and barged right into a gentleman, who was standing talking to a very elegantly dressed lady, and nearly knocked him flat.

'S sorry!' I gasped as we rocked to and fro in each other's embrace. 'Can't – stop! Must – catch – that – boy!'

Behind me came Toni's urgent voice.

'Veronique – I beg you! Veronique – *please*!' He put on a spurt and caught my arm. 'Please – I ask you to stop!'

I shook him off.

'Let me go, Toni! That beastly boy will get away!'

And then, right ahead, was the pond where the pelicans are kept, and I saw with delight that Hamish was making straight for it.

'Right-ho!' thought I grimly as I ran. 'Here's where you go for a swim, Hamish, my lad!' I urged my legs to run just a bit faster and, being the legs of a trained ballet dancer, they obeyed me. I caught up with Hamish just as he drew level with the pond, and gave him a push. Pelicans flew in all directions, uttering the funniest noises and flapping their ridiculous beaks. As for Hamish, he'd gone flat, and was now sitting up in one foot of water, wondering what had happened to him. Water dripped from his red hair and ran out of his large ears. It even oozed out of his mouth. He looked for all the world like a very disreputable dolphin or a statue for Father Neptune!

From near at hand came the angry voice of a keeper, and in another moment my arm was seized.

'Hi, miss! What d'you think you're doing, eh? How dare you push the young gentleman in that there pond! Now don't you go denying it, or saying it was a naccident, for I saw you do it.'

'I'm not denying it!' I yelled indignantly. 'And he's not a young gentleman. He's a cruel, horrible little boy! He gave my monkey a lighted cigarette, and he's crying – Jacko, I mean. It's Hamish who ought to be made to cry. He *deserves* a ducking!'

The keeper looked nonplussed. Then, fortunately for me, Toni came dashing up and began to explain.

'It is true,' said Toni. 'The boy did give the monkey a cigarette which was lighted. The little creature was cruelly hurt. You must certainly give the boy in charge, Keeper. My friend here' – he indicated me – 'my friend has a strong sense of justice. She was determined to see that he did not escape. I think she was, as you say in English, a little of the sport!'

'Ah, now that's altogether different, sir,' said the keeper, letting me go and looking respectfully at Toni, who, I must say, had a way with him when it came to dealing with officials. 'If the lad 'as been ill-treating anythink in this 'ere Zoo, now that's altogether different. It is that! Wot 'ave you got to say for yourself, me lad?' he added, turning to Hamish, who, I must say, looked the picture of guilt.

'How was I to know the silly creature would go putting it into its silly mouth?' muttered Hamish truculently. 'I thought it would just play with it.'

'You ain't got no business to go thinking at all,' declared the keeper severely. 'You oughta stop outside this 'ere Zoo, you ought, if you can't 'elp ill-treating the hanimals in it. It's somethink that oughta be put a stop to, and I thank you, sir' – he nodded to Toni – 'for puttin' me on to it.'

'Oh – er – that is quite all right,' murmured Toni, and as he said it I could see him working out the keeper's last words in his mind, wondering how you would analyse the sentence and making a mental note about the queerness of the English language! 'I had better take Miss Weston along to the ladies' cloakroom, had I not? She looks rather the worse for the wear, do you not think? Come, Veronique—' He took my arm firmly, and tried to lead me away.

'Wait a moment, Toni,' I said doggedly. 'What about Hamish?'

'You just leave 'im to me, miss,' said the keeper with a grin. 'I'll take care of 'im, and enjoy doing it! Come along, me lad!' He beckoned to the dripping Hamish, who had by this time issued forth from the pond and was standing in a rapidly growing pool on the path. 'Come along, you!'

I was thrilled to think that, all through me, Hamish had descended from being a 'young gentleman' to a mere 'lad' – in the keeper's eyes, anyway!

'You know, Veronique,' said Toni as we made our way to the nearest cloakroom, 'I wish most particularly for you to stop just now. I wish very much to introduce you to those people.'

'What?' I said. 'Oh, you mean that gentleman I barged into just now? Well, I'm most awfully sorry if he was a friend of yours, Toni, but really he shouldn't have stood right in my way. I simply couldn't *help* barging into him, now could I?'

'It was unfortunate,' said Toni gravely, but with a hint of laughter in his voice, 'because it will most certainly go down in your biography, Veronique. I see it in the eye of my friend, Oscar Deveraux.'

For a moment the name didn't mean anything. Then it dawned upon me.

'You don't – you can't mean *the* Oscar Deveraux?'

'Exactly,' answered Toni with a smile. '*The* Oscar Deveraux, as you put it. The author and ballet critic. This is what he will say of you when you become famous: "I remember Veronique Weston when she was a young girl. I met her in the Zoological Gardens – or rather it would be more accurate to say that I have her barge into me! I see her push an unfortunate youth into the pond of the pelican – not by accident, mind you, but by the design!"'

'Do stop being silly!' I giggled, 'and tell me who the lady was. I mean the lady who was with Oscar Deveraux.'

'Oh, that was his wife, Irma Foster, the ballerina,' Toni said casually. 'As I say, I wish to introduce you, Veronique, only you will not stop.'

'Oh, *Toni*!' I wailed. 'Where are they? Let's go and find them! Come quickly!'

'It is already too late,' said Toni with a smile. 'They are gone since a long time. And I think it is well that they are. Your appearance, my dear Veronique, is not prepossessing! I think if Oscar Deveraux were to see you now, your appearance, too, would go down in your biography!'

'Perhaps you're right,' I admitted. 'I expect I do look a bit of a wreck!'

After I had made myself presentable we went to the café beside the Snake House, and drank each other's health in lemon squash. The waitress brought us a plate of cakes and another of chocolate biscuits, and I'm afraid we ate the lot, only keeping one of the latter for Jacko. Outside the café, there was an ice-cream man, and Toni bought me a cornet.

We went home by way of the mandrills' cages, and poor Jacko was still crouched at the back of his cage, refusing to come out. He wouldn't even come out to take half a banana from a little girl who had several in a bag. When he saw me, though, he came at once; and when I offered him the end of my cornet he took it. I noticed that he smelt it very carefully before putting it into his mouth. Jacko had learnt something from the affair of the cigarette – and that was not to trust human beings!

Chapter 8

End of Term

THE last week of term flew by, and, almost before I knew it, it was Wednesday -- only three days before the holidays began. The people who were to be in the Finsbury Park Youth Festival were all very excited. It was awful, having them dashing into the dressing-room, tallking a hundred to the dozen about Miss Jackson of the Theatre Ballet, what she'd said and done, and to know that you were going to take no part in it.

'We're going to do *Les Sylphides*,' Sara said, as we got ready for class that afternoon. 'Sandra Vane is to do the Waltz, and Jessica Todd and John Godolphin the *pas-de-deux*. That's for the classical ballet. Then we're to do the Czardas from *Coppélia*, to show them what a national dance is like, and Carmen is doing one of her wriggly, Spanish dances with castanets and a swirling skirt. Lulu is doing Danse Arabe from *Le Casse Noisette*, and we finish with the Dance of the Little Swans from *Lac*. The Swans are June, Lily, Delia, and me. Then, at the end of the ballet part of the programme, we're to give a short demonstration of classical technique ... Oh, Veronica, what a shame you're not going to be in it! It's going to be such *fun*!'

'Oh, well,' I said with a sigh, 'I'll be able to go home for the hols, anyway, which I shouldn't be able to do if I were in the Youth Festival. I shall think of all of you working away at rehearsals while I'm riding on the moors. I had a letter from my cousin this morning.'

'Gosh! Have you got a pony all of your own?' asked June. 'You lucky thing!'

I shook my head.

'No, he doesn't really belong to me,' I admitted. 'But you

see, my cousins have both got ponies, and Sebastian – he's a boy cousin of theirs – well, he rides too, so I just had to have a mount. We tried a donkey first, but that wasn't awfully successful, because he wouldn't go unless Sebastian walked behind him with a stick and whacked him! In the end we had a Wayside Stall to make some money to hire a pony for me. The man we hired him from said that we could hang on to him until he wanted him. So far he hasn't wanted him,' I added.

'What's his name?' Sara demanded.

'Arabesque,' I said.

'What a lovely name for a pony!' exclaimed Taiis. 'It is one that I have never heard before. But, of course, you would call him something like that, Veronica – something to do with the dance, I mean. You are so one way of the mind! Always the dancing it is with you!'

As I sat in the train that night I took out Caroline's letter and read it through again. She wrote as follows:

Bracken Hall,
Bracken,
Northumberland.

Dear Veronica,

It seems ages since you went away, although I know it isn't so long really. I'm sorry I haven't written more, but you know how it is – school takes up so much time. It'll be glorious when the holidays are here, and there's time to do all the really important things, like grooming Gillyflower, and riding on the moors with Sebastian. Sebastian came home from school for half-term, and we rode right up to Corbie's Nob just to celebrate the occasion. Sebastian stood right on the very top of the cairn and said – you know his dramatic way; you never can tell whether he's serious or not! – 'Shades of Veronica! 'Twas here she set her foot upon the treacherous snake. Oh, hapless day! Oh, thrice-happy snake to be trodden upon by the foot of a world-famous ballet-dancer-to-be!'

Fiona is frightfully grown up, now that she's gone to her Harrogate school. She's got a long party frock, and I suppose she does look rather beautiful in it. She's had her hair permed, too – much to Sebastian's disgust – and she uses lipstick, though she says it isn't allowed at school – only in the Sixth Form for evenings. She went to the Hunt Dance at half-term, and who do you guess took her? Sebastian has broken up early, and he's looking over my shoulder as I write this letter. He says just think of the rottenest little trick you know, and you'll be right! I expect by now you've guessed. It was that awful Ian Frazer!

Sebastian has gone away at last and left me in peace, so I can tell you some news about *him*! He's going to leave school next term, and he's working like mad at his music. He spends simply *all his time* playing either the piano or the violin, and I have a frightful job persuading him to come out for an occasional ride! He's started a music club in Newcastle, and he says he's written a symphony. It's called the *Woodland Symphony*, and he's going to conduct it himself at a concert during the hols. I expect it will be while you're here. I think it won't be long before he tries for his scholarship to the Royal College of Music.

Would you believe it, but Mummy has got quite keen about ballet. I think she imagines it's fashionable! Anyway, she goes about telling people about 'my niece at Sadler's Wells'! Really, to hear her talk, you'd think you were a *prima ballerina* already! I heard her telling Mrs Musgrave the other day at a Woman's Institute meeting that her niece, Veronica's, dancing wasn't the ordinary kind that you see in musical comedies and pantomimes, but a *much* more difficult and superior kind! Mrs Musgrave looked most impressed, and I heard her say: 'Really, Mrs Scott? You *must* be proud of her!' Then Mummy smiled smugly, and said: 'Yes, I am a little proud, Mrs Musgrave. You see, it was really through *me* that Veronica was discovered. You re-member dear Lady Blantosh's concert? Well ...' Then Mummy went on telling Mrs Musgrave all about you dan-cing at the matinée and Madame Viret turning up, and your audition at Sadler's Wells, and by the time she'd finished, you'd really have supposed that *Mummy* had invited Madame to the matinée especially to discover you! You know Mummy when once she gets into her stride!'

I couldn't help laughing out loud as I read this bit. Yes, I did know Aunt June and her infuriating way of taking all the credit to herself. All the same, she was kind, as the next part of the letter showed.

Mummy is enclosing a cheque for your train fare next weekend. She says will you be sure to book a first-class sleeper because she doesn't like the idea of you travelling third, as you did when you came to stay with us first.

Sebastian says he's going to groom and exercise Arab-esque for you, so that he'll be in the pink of condition by the time you get here on Saturday night.

Much love from Caroline.

P.S. Mummy says she'll send Perkins with the car to meet you on Saturday. And, by the way, Lady Blantosh is having another concert on Boxing Day, and she wants you to dance at it.'

I laughed when I read the bit about the first-class sleeper. I believe Aunt June thought that no one except thieves and robbers travelled third class!

As I came out from the Underground at Chalk Farm I met Stella, and we walked to the bus together. I saw quite a lot of Stella nowadays. She didn't seem to have a great deal to do, and when I asked her the reason, she smiled ruefully.

'I never seem to get much beyond understudying people,'

she answered. 'In fact, the only real part I've had since I joined the Company has been one of the Black Lackeys in *The Gods Go A-Begging*, and *then* I got into an awful row because I lost my wig.'

'Lost your wig?' I echoed, fully alive to the seriousness of the admission. It's an awful crime to lose or destroy stage property. 'How on earth did you do that, Stella? I thought you were frightfully careful about your things.'

'So I am,' agreed Stella, a puzzled frown creasing her forehead. 'I simply can't think how it happened. I'm positive I put it away all right after I'd had it at the last performance, and how it came to be perched on the swan's head – you know, the mechanical swan they have in *Lac des Cygnes*? – well, how it came to be there in the wings at all, I just can't imagine.'

I couldn't help laughing. It must have looked so queer to see that dignified old swan wearing a curly black wig! But poor Stella was far from being amused.

'It's all very well for you to laugh, Veronica, but it was the night Madame was there, and she was *furious*. When Marcia yelled out: "Oh, *there's* Stella's wig – the one she lost," and Madame turned round and saw it, I thought I'd be dismissed on the spot!'

'Marcia?' I said thoughtfully. 'Now I wonder...'

'What's the matter?' asked Stella.

I didn't answer for a moment. I was thinking back in my mind to that day when Madame was supposed to have taken the class, and I'd found my tights in Mrs Wopping's bowl of dirty water. Also Sara's story about Delia's fishnet ones.

'Look here, Stella,' I said urgently, 'you must watch your step with Marcia Rutherford. She's the sort of girl who would stop at nothing to put a spoke in the wheel of a rival – nothing!'

'You think she put my wig there on purpose?' said Stella in amazement.

'I don't *think*; I know she did,' I pronounced. 'Well, you just watch out, Stella, or you'll find yourself stepping out of your parts, and Marcia Rutherford stepping into them! Take my word for it!'

Stella didn't answer because just at that moment our bus came, and we had to keep our place in the long queue that had formed while we were waiting.

'It's the end of term on Friday,' I said when we had taken our seats. 'I'm going to Northumberland to stay with my cousins.'

Stella gave a funny little sigh.

'Northumberland – it makes me think of hills and moors, with no sound except the sheep cropping the grass, and fir woods with the bracken knee-deep – lovely!' she said dreamily.

'What? In November!' I laughed.

'When I think of Northumberland, I always think of bracken and heather, and the curlews calling,' said Stella. 'Sometimes I wonder—'

I never knew what she wondered, for just at that moment the conductor came for our tickets.

'Talking of holidays,' I went on after he had gone, 'Jonathan thought we ought to have a sort of breaking-up dinner party. Actually, we don't break up till Friday, but, as I'm going north by the night train, we thought it might be a bit of a rush if we had it then, so we're having it on Thursday. That's tomorrow. You see, somebody in the country sent Jonathan a brace of pheasants, and, as he says, they're no earthly use to him as he's a vegetarian. He can't even make a still-life of them because they're all plucked and trussed up! So he's given them to Mrs Crapper for our party. And Mrs Crapper made two Christmas puddings, and now she says she'll only need one, with me away, so we're having the second one for our party. Isn't it perfectly sweet of her?'

'Yes – she is a dear soul,' agreed Stella. 'Really, I don't know what any of us would do without her.'

'Or Jonathan either,' I put in firmly. 'They're *his* pheasants, you know.'

'Or Jonathan either,' laughed Stella. 'Well, I've a party of my own on Thursday night. Some ballet club or other are giving it, and they've asked the whole Company as guests. Well, a lot of them say they can't be bothered to go, but I think it'll be frightfully disappointing for the ballet club, so I've said I'll turn up. Oh, it's all right – it's not till nine o'clock,' she added, seeing my downcast face, 'so I'll be able to come to the dinner party first. There'll be loads of time.'

'You're sure?' I said anxiously. 'Jonathan will be fearfully disappointed if you don't turn up, Stella.'

'I'll come,' promised Stella. 'At seven o'clock I'll be there.'

Chapter 9

Mrs Crapper Has a Dinner Party

OUR dinner party was a great success. We had it in Mrs Crapper's sitting-room (she called it simply 'the room'), and we sat at the round centre table which was covered by an enormous damask tablecloth, especially brought out for the occasion. It had been Mrs Crapper's mother's best tablecloth when *she* was married. In the middle of the white expanse was a square of looking-glass meant to look like a lake, and on the lake floated a white china swan that Mrs Crapper had won at a hoopla stall in Margate. The swan was filled with ivy leaves that Jonathan had gathered (under Mrs Crapper's orders) from the wall of the yard at the back of the house, and there were trails of ivy at various places all over the table 'to give a artistic effect', as Mrs Crapper put it!

Besides the pheasants and the Christmas pudding, Mrs Crapper had brought out a bottle of home-made ginger wine which we drank in wineglasses all of different sizes and patterns because Mrs Crapper had won them at a hoopla stall, too. It occurred to me that Mrs Crapper had Margate to thank for quite a lot of her household furnishings! We had white sauce with the plum pudding, with brandy in it out of the medicine chest.

After we'd finished, Jonathan asked permission to light his old black pipe, and we roasted chestnuts over the fire, ate almonds and raisins, told funny stories, and tried to make-believe that it was really Christmas. Stella didn't smoke, because it's not good for your breathing, and neither did I, as I was too young, and anyway the same reason applied to me, even if I hadn't been.

At eight o'clock Stella went upstairs to get ready for her

party. She wore a black taffeta picture frock that she'd made herself. It was ankle-length, and it had a lace yoke and cuffs, and huge bouffant sleeves. With her fair hair brushed back into a shining 'page-boy', and her little pointed chin, she looked exactly like a painting by an Old Master. Jonathan took her to the bus. He said he never *could* believe that Stella was capable of looking after herself.

When he came back, Jonathan said we'd have a symphony concert in Mrs Crapper's kitchen while we washed up the dinner dishes, and away he dashed up the four flights of stairs to his own floor to get his portable gramophone.

'I'll carry down the records!' I yelled, following on behind rather more slowly. 'Let's put on the whole of *Lac des Cygnes*, and that lovely thing by Prokofieff – *Peter and the Wolf*. Oh, and let's have—'

I stopped suddenly. Jonathan had swung wide the door of his studio, and there, facing me, was a large picture. It stood on an easel, and I had seen it many times. But whereas before it had always been covered by a piece of old black velvet, now it was triumphantly displayed. It was a picture of a ballet dancer. She was seated, backstage, on a piece of scenery, tying her shoe which had come loose, her head was bent down, and her fair hair was falling all over her neck and shoulders in soft abandon.

A shadowy figure in the background, evidently her partner, was surveying her sardonically.

Suddenly, something in the turn of the neck, the way the soft hair grew, seemed familiar to me.

'Why – why, it's *Stella*!' I cried in astonishment. 'When did you paint it, Jonathan? I didn't know Stella had ever sat for you.'

'Oh, yes,' smiled Jonathan. 'Stella has sat for me many times. She sat for this while you were away, living with your cousins. I haven't shown it to you because it wasn't finished, and I wanted it to be a surprise. Do you like it, Veronica?'

'Like it?' I echoed. '"Like" is quite the wrong word. I think it's *wonderful*, Jonathan.'

Jonathan made me a mock bow.

'Thank you, Veronica.'

I stared at the picture, fascinated. The subject might be ordinary enough, but the execution was anything but common-place. The girl's flesh was a beautiful creamy colour and seemed so real that you felt it would be warm to the touch. There was a luminous quality about the dress and the hair, that shone out of the shadowy background with an almost un-earthly radiance. The youth and softness of the dancer con-trasted vividly with the sardonic expression of her partner, and the sordidness of her stage surroundings.

'Have you sold it, Jonathan?' I asked. 'What are you going to do with it?'

'I'm going to keep it for myself,' Jonathan told me. 'But first it's going to be in the Spring Exhibition of Young British Painters at the Monmouth Gallery.'

'Golly!' I breathed. 'The Monmouth Gallery! You *are* get-ting famous, Jonathan!'

'Oh, I expect they had a job to find suitable canvases,' Jona-than said modestly. 'And, by the way, I have another picture here that's going to be in the same exhibition.' He drew for-ward a small canvas that had been standing with its face to the wall. 'Remember this?'

The picture facing me was of a small, pale-faced little girl, sitting on the extreme edge of a chair. One foot was wearing a darned sock, and the other a very old and battered canvas ballet shoe. There was a frown of concentration on the child's face as she painstakingly darned the shoe in her hand.

'Why, it's *me*!' I said. 'It's that picture you did of me, Jonathan, ages ago. Gosh! What a plain child I used to be!'

'Plain, but interesting,' said Jonathan with a smile. '*I* thought so, anyway. In the exhibition it will be called: "Study of a Dancer", because it isn't the fashion to give pictures names. Privately, though, I call it: "A Dancer Takes a Holiday!"'

'Yes, it's perfectly true,' I said, smiling at the irony of the title. 'An awful lot of our so-called free time *is* spent in darning shoes, washing tights, ironing tunics, and so forth.'

'And yet you still like doing it?' said Jonathan, pulling out the gramophone from the bottom of the cupboard and dumping a pile of records in my arms. 'You still think a ballet dancer's life worth living?'

'Of course I do,' I answered. 'It's a *wonderful* life – at least, it is when things go well.'

Jonathan switched off the light of his attic studio and shut the door behind him.

'U-um,' he said dubiously. 'It seems to me to be no sort of life at all for a girl. What about when you fall in love and want to get married?'

'I shan't ever fall in love,' I pronounced. 'I shall be "wedded to my art".'

'So you say – at sixteen. Or is it fifteen?' said Jonathan, dumping down the gramophone on Mrs Crapper's kitchen table, all among the dirty dinner dishes. 'But when you're *really* old – say, twenty-six, like me – you may think differently. What do *you* say, Martha?'

Mrs Crapper wiped her hands carefully on the overall that she wore on special occasions in place of a common or garden apron. Then she clamped into the sitting-room, took up a photograph in a green plush frame that stood on what she called 'me occasional table', came back with it, and stood for a moment gazing at it lovingly. The photograph showed a weak-chinned little man with a drooping walrus moustache and watery eyes. This was he whom Mrs Crapper called her 'better half'. Personally, I thought the term slightly misleading, since Mr Crapper had undoubtedly gone to the dogs – literally, as well as the other way! After gambling away every penny of his wife's hard-earned savings, he had finally taken himself off, in the company of a flashily dressed female who carried a croco-

78

dile handbag nearly as big as herself and wore an imitation diamond ring that was a close rival to the Koh-i-noor.

'Well,' said Mrs Crapper with a gusty sigh, 'I always say, when I thinks of poor Crapper, it's better to 'ave loved and lorst than never to 'ave loved at all. That's wot I says.'

'You're right there, Martha,' said Jonathan, winding up the gramophone and putting on the first record of *Swan Lake*. 'Dead right. There's only one thing to beat your theory, Martha, and that's to have loved and *not* lost.' He picked up a tea-towel and began to dry the dishes that Mrs Crapper had put on a tin tray to drain, while I followed suit.

'Ah,' said Mrs Crapper, with another look at the photograph, 'but it's only when you've lorst, Mr Jonathan, that you realizes the pearl of great price that was giv' you till death you do part. Only,' she added with yet another sigh, 'it weren't death, but dogs, that parted Crapper and me.'

So saying, Mrs Crapper wiped the soapsuds off her workworn hands and replaced the erring Mr Crapper on the 'occasional' table in the sitting-room, and with this last gesture she put her romantic past behind her.

'And now,' she said in her ordinary voice, 'how about a nice box of liquorice all-sorts to cheer us up?'

At about ten o'clock I said I thought I'd go to bed, because I was tired and wanted a good night's sleep before my long journey north.

Jonathan said he'd sit up with Mrs Crapper and listen to the wireless, if she didn't mind; then he'd hear Stella come in.

'She won't be late,' I assured him. 'She's got a dress rehearsal tomorrow, and the opening performance of the new ballet they're doing down at the Wells. That's something you can't do if you're a ballet dancer – stay out late at parties!'

Chapter 10

Stella Disappears

CLASSES were just as usual next day. Character finished at five, and soon after that I was racing homewards. The holidays had begun! I had oceans of time, really, as I had packed my things yesterday, and my sleeper was booked.

I arrived at the door of 242 Heather Hill exactly as the postman got there with the evening post. There was a sale catalogue for Mrs Crapper, a registered parcel for Jonathan, and, to my astonishment, a letter addressed to me in Stella's big, open handwriting. I opened it as I walked upstairs, after leaving Mrs Crapper's catalogue on her table, wondering what on earth Stella could have to write to me about, when she'd promised to come to the station to see me off before her performance. When I had read the first few lines I wondered no longer.

'My darling Veronica,' [said the pencilled scrawl]. 'I don't know what you'll think when you know what I've done – or rather what I'm going to do. Actually it's another hour before I shall do it, and that's why I'm writing you such a long letter.

For ages I've been feeling terribly depressed. When I got into the Company I thought things might be better, but very soon I knew that it wasn't any use. You see, I can't push myself forward like some people can; it just doesn't seem nice to get to the front that way. But there's no denying the fact – a bit of push gets you there quicker than any amount of hard work, and if you can manage to put in a bit of the latter, and push as well, then you'll have the world at your feet in no time!

As I told you a bit ago, Belinda and Marcia are getting all the parts that ought by rights to be mine. Of course, Belinda *is* wonderful, but Marcia – well, she's not even in the Company yet, and I know quite well that I can dance lots better than she can, but she manages to convince the Powers-That-Be that she's the best, and I expect the audience thinks so too. There's an awful lot in showmanship, as Gilbert is so fond of telling us! Anyway, there you are; they get the parts, and I understudy them!

After you'd gone this morning, just before I had to set off for rehearsal, a letter came from Granny. Of course, I knew she'd been ill, but the writing was all thin and shaky; she must have been an awful lost worse than she said to have written like that. Oh, Veronica – why have people got to grow old and die – people one loves? It's so cruel! You see, I haven't got anyone else to care what becomes of me – only Granny, and she's over eighty.

Suddenly, as I was passing King's Cross Station, I knew what I was going to do. I wasn't going to that rehearsal; I wasn't going to a rehearsal ever any more; I was going to walk on to the northbound train, and go back to Granny to look after her for as long as she lived. And that's why I'm sitting here in the waiting-room, writing this letter.

Goodbye, darling Veronica, from your

unhappy Stella.

PS. I can't help thinking how queer it is that it should be *me*, of all people, who should walk out on the Sadler's Wells Ballet. I don't suppose anyone – I mean anyone in the mere *corps-de-ballet* – has ever done it before, but I know quite well in my heart that my contract won't be renewed, so I've only got in my thrust first.

PPS. I'm very sorry not to be able to wait and travel with you, Veronica, but you see I happen to know that you've got a first-class ticket, and the exchequer just won't run to it. Besides, if I wait, I may be a coward and change my mind.

Tell Jonathan he was quite right – I *am* a failure.

Of course, as soon as I had read the letter I flew up the stairs to Jonathan's studio.

'Jonathan!' I yelled. 'Jonathan! Stella's gone! She's gone home. Oh, not for a holiday – she's gone for good!'

Jonathan didn't seem to be nearly so amazed and put about by my shattering news as you'd have thought. He wiped his paintbrush carefully on a bit of rag, and said: 'Gone home, has she? About time she did!'

'But Jonathan—' I expostulated. 'You don't understand. She's gone *altogether*; she's left the ballet; she can never go back – not after walking out on them like this. Don't you understand, Jonathan? Oh, Jonathan – what are we to do?'

Jonathan stood up and stretched himself leisurely. Then he rummaged in his pockets for his ancient pipe.

'Look,' he said, when he'd found it and lit up. 'Honestly, Veronica, thinking it over calmly, do *you* think Stella is a fit person to spend her life fighting for a front place on the stage? Do you honestly think she'd make a go of it, or that she'd be happy even if she did?'

I met Jonathan's dark eyes, and I saw that the anxious look I had so often seen in them had disappeared. There was nothing in them now but relief.

'Y-es,' I said slowly, 'I see what you mean, Jonathan, and perhaps you're right. Stella is a bit – well, sort of gentle and retiring for a stage career. You've got to be tough as tough, and not let yourself get discouraged, whatever happens.' I thought of the awful things that had happened to me this term, and I sighed.

'Why the sigh?' questioned Jonathan.

'Sometimes it's dreadfully hard *not* to get discouraged,' I answered. Then I threw up my chin and added: 'But I'll manage it somehow. I refuse to let a girl like Marcia Rutherford get me down! I'm going to dance, and no one – no one is going to stop me! Certainly not Marcia Rutherford!'

'That's the spirit!' said Jonathan approvingly. 'It's people like you, Veronica, who ought to go on the stage – not North Country primroses like Stella.'

We were both silent for a long time. Presently there was a scraping sound at the window. Jonathan got up and opened the casement, whereupon a small but very important kitten of a bright yellow colour bounced in and began to rub itself against Jonathan's corduroy trousers in an ecstacy of affection. Really, it was almost impossible to believe that such resounding purrs could come from so small an animal.

'Good evening, Picasso!' Jonathan said solemnly, tickling the little creature under its chin. 'Just in time for a spot of condensed milk. I was about to open a tin for Veronica's coffee.'

The kitten belonged to the people next door, and its real name was Marmalade, but since it spent nine-tenths of its life in Jonathan's studio, he'd given it the rather more artistic name of Picasso, not out of any disrespect to the artist, as he carefully explained, but just because its fur reminded him of Picasso's passion for primary colours!

We sat drinking the coffee Jonathan had made, and we were both so deep in our own thoughts that neither of us spoke for a long time. Picasso meanwhile proceeded to make short work of the condensed milk that Jonathan had poured into a saucer for him.

'But what are we going to do about Stella?' I said after a bit. 'We can't just say "that's that!" and never see her again, can we?'

'Rather not!' agreed Jonathan cheerfully. 'I have no intention of not seeing Stella again. Not the least intention in the world, I assure you. In fact, I'm coming along with you this very night, Veronica, to follow Stella to her home in far-off Northumberland.'

'Northumberland?' I echoed in astonishment. 'You don't mean to say that Stella lives in Northumberland?'

'Oh, yes,' said Jonathan. 'At least her granny does. She lives in a little village at the foot of the Cheviot Hills. Didn't you know?'

I shook my head.

'Of course, I knew her home was somewhere up north, because you kept on calling her "a North Country primrose", but I alway thought of places like Manchester, or Leeds. But if she lives in the heart of the Cheviots, as you say, where on earth did she learn to dance?'

'Ah, you see, she didn't live there then,' explained Jonathan. 'She used to live with her mother, not so very far from Darlington, and that's where she learned to dance, I suppose. Then, when her mother died, Stella came to London. In the holidays she went home to her granny at Broomyhough.'

'You seem to know an awful lot about Stella,' I said thoughtfully.

Jonathan puffed away at his pipe, while Picasso, having finished the milk, sprang upon his shoulder and playfully bit his ear.

'I've known Stella for a long time,' he said at length. 'When she came here first she was only a kid of fourteen, and I was just twenty-two and still a student at the Slade. By the way, I'm North Country myself, you know.'

I stared at Jonathan in amazement. I had always thought of him being born within sound of Bow Bells.

'You, Jonathan?'

'Oh, yes,' smiled Jonathan. 'My people come from a village called Ravenskirk, near the Scottish border.'

'*Now* I know why your voice always sounded queer to me!' I exclaimed. 'Queer, yet sort of familiar. It was the faint burr that all North Country people have, and never seem to lose, no matter how long they stay away from home. But you never said you lived in Northumberland,' I added reproachfully. 'Not even last year, when you knew I was going to live there.'

'I forgot all about it,' Jonathan declared. 'Matter of fact, I never go home, so it didn't signify.'

'You are queer, Jonathan,' I said. 'What is your home like, anyway? Is it a big house?'

'Oh, so-so,' he answered.

'Yes, but is it *big*?' I persisted. 'Or is it a teeny-weeny cottage?'

'Just a house,' Jonathan said noncommittally, and I knew by past experience that he didn't intend to say any more. 'By the way, it's seven o'clock. Hadn't we better trek down to Martha, and break the news to her that one of her birds has flown, and that the other two are sitting on the telegraph wires preparing to migrate! She might take pity on us, and give us some real supper to speed us on our journey! I shall have to ring up King's Cross, too, and see if they can give me a sleeper.'

'Oh, by the way, Jonathan,' I said uncomfortably, 'you know my Uncle John and Aunt June are disgustingly well off?'

Jonathan nodded.

'I'd gathered that fact.'

'Well, Aunt June sent me the money for my ticket,' I went on. 'A first-class sleeper. It – it was *frightfully* expensive.'

'Thanks for the tactful warning, Veronica,' Jonathan said with a grin. 'All the same, I think I'll travel first class too, and act the knight-errant. After all, I don't do *much* travelling.'

'Perhaps I could change over to third class—' I began, but Jonathan stopped me with a wave of his hand.

'Not at all, my dear Veronica. We'll *both* travel first class on this historic occasion. After all, it will give me an opportunity of studying the habits of the idle rich! Useful for a struggling artist! I might be able to turn out a satirical masterpiece in the vein of Hogarth, and call it: "Night Life on the Flying Scotsman"!'

'You may not get the sleeper,' I said with a giggle. 'You may have to go third with the thieves and vagabonds!'

Chapter 11

Journey to Northumberland

BUT Jonathan was lucky. Someone had cancelled a sleeper booking at the last minute, so at exactly eleven forty-five we made our way up the long platform at King's Cross Station to the first-class sleeping car, and boarded the northbound train. The sleeping-car attendant took our luggage and ushered us along the corridor to our respective compartments and left us with the assurance that he'd bring us tea at seven forty-five in the morning.

'Gosh, Jonathan!' I said, stopping short on the threshold of my compartment, 'I never imagined a first-class sleeper was like this! Why, it's a real little bedroom with a proper bed, and a washbasin with hot and cold water!'

'We live and learn!' said Jonathan, with a flash of his white teeth. 'Well, goodnight, Veronica! See you at crack of dawn in Newcastle. By the way, I suppose they're sending someone to meet you?'

'Oh, yes – Perkins!' I said with a grimace. 'Aunt June said I was to wait for him in the tea-room. He's the Scotts' chauffeur. Do you get out at Newcastle too, Jonathan?'

'Yes, that's as far as this train goes,' he answered. 'I get another one later in the day to Rothbury; then a bus to Alwynton, and from there I expect I walk!'

'It sounds lovely,' I said.

I must have been very tired, for I slept soundly, not even waking at Grantham or York. When I opened my eyes it was very early in the morning, and the train was slowly sliding through a station. I pulled back the blind a little, and saw the towers and spires of Durham Castle and Cathedral, shining in the frosty moonlight like a fairy city. A puff of cold North Country air came in through the window which was open a little at the top.

I gave a shiver, half of cold and half of excitement. Then I snuggled under my eiderdown again, because, although we were only twenty minutes' journey from Newcastle, I knew that we didn't have to leave the train for ages yet.

I remembered the last time I had seen Durham. It had been in broad daylight, over eighteen months ago, and I had been sitting in the corridor of this very train, talking to Sebastian. I'd thought, then, how cold and alien it looked; now, I was greeting it as an old friend, which just shows how your ideas can change in a short time.

The next time I woke it was after seven o'clock, and we were in Newcastle. By the time I had washed and dressed, it was half past seven, and the attendant was at the door with my tea and a biscuit. Jonathan came down the corridor, cup in hand, and we had our tea together, sitting on my bed.

'How long shall you be staying at – I forget the name of the village where you said Stella lives?' I asked him.

'Broomyhough,' answered Jonathan. 'I shall only stay a couple of days, I expect.'

'It seems a long journey for just a couple of days,' I said. 'Couldn't you stay a bit longer, now you're here, Jonathan?'

'I might – who knows?' Jonathan answered slowly, breaking his biscuit into four and putting them all into his mouth at one go. 'It all depends upon how Stella receives me.'

'Oh, Stella will receive you with open arms,' I assured him. 'She's awfully fond of you, Jonathan.'

'That's what I'm going to find out,' Jonathan declared. 'I want to know just how much Stella thinks of me. If she can't bear the sight of me, I shall come back by the night train tomorrow; if she thinks I'm not *quite* a blot on the landscape, I shall stay for as long as she and her granny will put up with me.'

'You'll be here for an awful long time, then, I'm thinking!'
I laughed.

At exactly eight o'clock I went along to the tea-room as
arranged. Jonathan came too, and hovering behind was our
porter, carrying my small suitcase and the large, square hatbox
of plywood that Jonathan had made to hold my ballet dress.
The latter wasn't heavy, but it was awkward to carry, so Jonathan had insisted upon the porter. Standing just within the
door of the tea-room were two well-known figures.

'Sebastian, and Caroline!' I shrieked. 'How lovely of you
both to come and meet me!'

'Well, we thought the impeccable Perkins might afford
rather a chilly welcome!' said Sebastian solemnly. 'It wasn't
that we were at all anxious to see *you*, Veronica.'

'Don't take any notice of him!' laughed Caroline. 'He's just
as batty as ever! The truth is, it was great fun getting up in
the middle of the night! Gosh, Veronica -- it's wonderful to
see you again! You look quite different -- lots more grown up,
and -- and prettier.'

'I feel just the same,' I laughed.

'Did you have a good journey?' went on Caroline. 'I think it
must be great fun to travel by sleeper.'

'Oh, it was frightfully comfortable,' I declared. 'It was just
like travelling in your own bedroom. And, of course, I had
Jonathan with me -- oh, by the way, where *is* Jonathan? He
was here just a moment ago.' I looked round the tea-room, but
Jonathan had vanished.

'Bloke with a beard?' queried Sebastian. 'When he saw
Caroline and me, he decided he didn't like the look of us, and
hopped it.'

'Don't be ridiculous!' I said, taking him seriously. 'Of
course, Jonathan would like both of you. Oh, how annoying! I
did so want you to meet.'

'Well, it's no use wishing,' said Sebastian. 'He's gone, and
that's that. Funny, but I always imagined your Jonathan as a
middle-aged sort of chap. Why, he seemed quite young!'

'Jonathan is twenty-six,' I said.

'He's not exactly my idea of an artist,' went on Sebastian, 'except for the board. I always imagined artists to be rangy sort of chaps – thin, and knock-kneed, with a hungry expression.'

I couldn't help laughing. It wasn't a bit like Jonathan!

'Well, come on; let's be going,' said Caroline. 'We left Perkins outside in the car, and he'll be getting impatient. We've brought some sandwiches and a flask of coffee, and we can have them on the way home; it'll be better than this place.' She cast a disparaging glance at the marble-topped counter with its piles of doorstep sandwiches, and thick, chipped cups of greasy coffee.

We had a picnic breakfast in the car, and I must say that for once I really appreciated the smoothly running, palatial Rolls, with its pull-out table and picnic cups and caucers.

'I'll bet this is the first time these things have ever been used,' Sebastian remarked, filling up my cup with hot coffee. 'Aunt June doesn't approve of picnics; she thinks they're beneath her – morally, as well as in actual fact!'

'Well, most grown-ups prefer meals on tables,' Caroline said loyally.

'Most, but not all,' declared Sebastian. 'My father is as keen on picnics as anyone.'

'D'you mind if I put my head out of the roof?' I asked, when he had finished the coffee and the sandwiches. 'Oh, look – there's that funny bit of Roman Wall at Heddon! Gosh! Doesn't it smell wonderful!'

'What – the Roman Wall?' said Sebastian. 'Shouldn't have thought the smell would have lasted all this time! Anyway, those Roman johnnies were very clean, if you can go by what you read. They did nothing but bath, day and night!'

'I didn't mean the Wall, you idiot! I meant everything generally.'

'Just smell to me,' drawled Sebastian. 'On the chilly side, too.'

'That's just what's so marvellous about it,' I declared. 'When you've been breathing air full of petrol fumes, and dust, and other people, you can't imagine how *fresh* this smells. It's full of trees, and moors, and snow just round the corner.'

'You've said it!' agreed Sebastian. 'There's a cap of snow on Corbie's Nob.'

We turned right at the bottom of Brunton Bank, and sped along the Bellingham road. The queer thing about Bracken was that you could reach it by two different roads – either the Newcastle–Otterburn one, or the Bellingham one that we were now on.

The scenery got wilder, and the air keener. I was glad to let Sebastian shut the sliding-roof, and to snuggle down under the rugs. After all, it wasn't yet nine o'clock in the morning, and as Caroline said, the world wasn't aired – not the world of the Northumberland moors, anyway!

'I'm getting soft!' I said with a shiver. 'A ballet school is such a warm place, you know. Gilbert positively *raves* if anyone so much as opens a window! One day they had the painters in doing something to the Baylis Hall, and the men left the windows open to dry the paint. Gilbert slammed them shut and roared: "Do you men realize that these girls are *dancers*? That they must not be exposed to sudden draughts of cold air? That they may strain their muscles by exercising in a cold room? In other words," yelled Gilbert, "these windows must be kept *shut*!"

'The poor men went out, their tails between their legs, and I heard them murmuring things about "those poor girls, and that brute of a dancing master"!'

'Gosh! He does sound a bit of a dragon!' Caroline exclaimed.

'He's not a dragon at all – he's a perfect lamb,' I told her indignantly. 'It's just his way. He's temperamental; most *artistes* are.'

'And you feel you're getting on?' Sebastian asked. 'With your dancing, I mean?'

I considered for a few moments. Then I said slowly:

'I seem to have had a run of awful bad luck this term. First of all I missed the audition for the Youth Festival because my watch was slow. Then the very day I got into the *pas-de-deux* class Serge suddenly decided he wouldn't have any Juniors in it, so I'm *still* not in. Then Toni and I went to the Zoo and I barged into a Mr Deveraux and nearly knocked him flat.'

'Who's Mr Deveraux?' demanded Caroline.

'Oh, he's a *frightfully* important person,' I explained. 'He's a ballet critic, and Toni says he'll be sure to put it all down in my biography. Not that I shall ever be famous enough to have a biography,' I added. 'Still, it was awful—'

'Who is this Toni?' drawled Sebastian. 'I'm not sure I like the sound of him.'

'Oh, yes, you would,' I said emphatically. 'Everyone likes Toni – he's frightfully popular.'

'You haven't told us who the fellow is yet,' said Sebastian. 'Or how it was you were traipsing round the Zoo with him.'

'I wasn't traipsing!' I laughed. 'As a matter of fact it was Sunday morning, and we had members' tickets, so I was walking very sedately. At least I was until Hamish gave Jacko the cigarette—'

'Hold on a bit!' begged Sebastian. 'You seem to have been in the centre of a positive crowd of male admirers! Toni – Hamish – Jacko—'

I burst out laughing.

'Admirers! You *are* funny, Sebastian! Why, Jacko is my little monkey in the Zoo – I'm sure I've told you all about Jacko. And Hamish – gosh, you should just have seen Hamish after I pushed him in the pelicans' pond! Why, he—'

Then I told them all about the fight with Hamish, and the triumphant ending it had had. Caroline laughed so much that Perkins turned half round in the driving seat to see what all the row was about.

'The keeper called him "my lad" when I'd finished with

him,' I said triumphantly. 'So it all goes to show what you can do if you really set your mind to it.'

'You *still* haven't told us who this Toni fellow is,' grumbled Sebastian.

'Toni is my dancing partner,' I said. 'At least, he *was* my partner, but now he's been taken into the Company, and I don't expect I shall ever see him again. That's why we were at the Zoo that Sunday morning; we were having a goodbye party. Toni's not only a dancer – he's a choreographer. That's a person who makes up dances,' I added, in case they didn't know.

'Of course we know that,' declared Sebastian.

'Well, *I* didn't,' admitted Caroline. 'I thought it was a person who trimmed your toenails and cut off your corns!'

'That's a chiropodist, ignoramus,' said Sebastian. 'Well, you do seem to have had a cheerful term, Veronica – I *don't* think.'

'Oh, but I've enjoyed every minute of it,' I declared. 'All the things that went wrong were my own stupid fault. At least, I suppose they were. Anyway, I shall take jolly good care nothing like that happens to me next term. Everyone has bad luck sometimes. Stella – she's the girl who shares my sitting-room at Mrs Crapper's – well, Stella had a spot of bad luck, too. Her wig—' I stopped suddenly. With a shock I remembered the awful thing that had happened to Stella, and I shivered.

'What's the matter, Veronica?' queried Sebastian. 'You shivered! Has someone walked over your grave?'

I laughed.

'No – I was only just thinking.'

'Penny for them!' persisted Sebastian. 'They must have been queer thoughts by the peculiar expression on your face! Come on, Veronica; let's hear what they were.'

'No,' I said slowly, shaking my head. 'They were thoughts best kept to myself.'

'There's Daddy!' exclaimed Caroline, as a car passed us

with a hoot. 'He said he'd probably meet us about here. Go on, Veronica – you were telling us about your queer dancing school.'

'There's nothing more to tell,' I said, 'except that I seem to be just as far off the Lilac Fairy as ever – in fact, sometimes I feel further off. By the way,' I added, as we turned off the main road, 'how far is a place called Broomyhough from here?'

'You mean the Strong's place, north of Alwynton?' said Sebastian. 'Oh, not very far as the crow flies. About fifteen miles, I should say.'

'Yes, but I'm not a crow!' I laughed. 'How far is it the other way – I mean by the road?'

'Miles and miles,' put in Caroline. 'You see, there just isn't a road across from Bracken. It's open moorland, so you've got to go all the way back to Bellingham, and then get a bus along the Jedburgh road. Do you want to go there, Veronica?'

I nodded.

'Yes, you see . . .' Then I told them all about Stella and the awful thing that had happened about her stage career.

'And now that Jonathan has told me exactly where she lives, I feel I'd like to go and see her while I'm here,' I ended.

'Well, why not ride there?' suggested Sebastian. 'Better still – why not let's all ride there tomorrow? After all, what better could we do than go out riding, if it's a decent day?'

'Oh, that would be *lovely*!' I said, with a sigh of happiness at the thought. 'You don't know how I've ached for a gallop on Arabesque ever since I knew I was coming back here these holidays. You don't think it'll be too far, do you?'

'Not a bit of it,' declared Sebastian. 'We'll start at crack of dawn and take it in easy stages. Trixie will give us lunch and tea, and we can make a whole day of it.'

As we turned in at the gates leading to Bracken Hall I thought of that night, last autumn, when I had run away in the mist. How different everything had looked then!

'Gosh!' I exclaimed, 'the last time I saw these gates was when they loomed up out of the mist like – like—'

'The gallows,' supplied Sebastian cheerfully.

'I never even thought of such a horrible thing,' I declared. 'But now you come to mention it, Sebastian, they *did* look a bit sinister, especially with you standing in the middle of the road yelling: "Have at you! Your money or your life!" or whatever it was you did yell.'

I let down the window of the car so that I could see everything more clearly. Yes, it was all the same – the little cottage at the bottom of the drive where Sebastian lived, with its diamond-paned windows, and low, overhanging eaves where the swallows built their nests in the summertime; the lake with its ruffled grey waters, seen clearly now through the leafless trees; finally, the long, low house with the Northumbrian moors rising in steep folds at its back.

We went into the hall, and Perkins followed with my luggage. Someone was coming from the kitchen quarters – someone carrying a tray with a glass of orange juice on it.

'Trixie!' I shrieked. 'It's me! Veronica! I'm back! I'm home again!'

I flung my arms round her neck, and the orange juice – Fiona's orange juice – nearly went west. Sebastian saved it by taking it out of Trixie's hands and depositing it on a table nearby. Trixie had been my cousins' old nurse, and now she was Aunt June's housekeeper. 'Oh, Trixie – it's lovely to be back! Not that it isn't lovely in London, too, but it's so gorgeous to see you all again. Oh, hullo, Fiona!'

Fiona, my elder cousin, returned my greeting coldly. She had never really liked me, and I knew in my heart that she never would. Sebastian said that Fiona loved nobody but herself, and I couldn't help feeling that he was right.

'Is that Veronica?' said a voice from the top of the stairs – Aunt June's voice. 'Well, Veronica! And how are you? Just as pale as ever, I see, and not a bit fatter!' I felt this to be a compliment, though I knew that Aunt June didn't mean it as such.

'We've waited for breakfast,' Aunt June went on, kissing me. 'So just put your things in the cloakroom for now, dear, and come along.'

She led the way into the morning-room, and we followed. We had a real North Country breakfast – porridge with moist brown sugar and cream on it; home-fed bacon and new-laid eggs, and after that, toast and honey. We had coffee, made with milk, to drink. No wonder both Fiona and Caroline had lovely complexions, I thought! I couldn't help thinking of my own breakfast at Mrs Crapper's – baked beans on toast, or kippers more often than not, and weak tea.

Chapter 12

Bracken Hall Again

AFTER breakfast we went straight round to the stables. Sebastian had been as good as his word and had brought in Arabesque and groomed him. For the last week he'd been up at six o'clock every morning, Caroline told me, exercising him. I was full of gratitude to Sebastian when I looked at my beloved pony, so sleek and shining.

'He knows me, too,' I said, rubbing his nose. 'I expect he wondered what had happened to me when I left him at that farm in the mist and never came back to him. Wouldn't it be queer if we could tell what horses think?'

'Oh, I don't expect they think at all,' put in Fiona loftily. 'Horses are terribly stupid animals; they haven't any brains really – they're just creatures of habit.'

'Oh, I don't agree with you there,' Sebastian said, and then Fiona and he were off on one of their arguments. Fiona and Sebastian were always arguing, and if ever Sebastian could say anything that he knew would annoy Fiona, he did so. There wasn't much love lost between Sebastian and his cousin! I put it down partly to the fact that Fiona was living in the house that belonged to Sebastian, by rights – Sebastian's father being the eldest son – and partly that Sebastian and Fiona were so unlike by nature. Fiona hadn't the ghost of a sense of humour, whereas Sebastian was never serious – not outwardly, anyway.

'I'll come out riding with you this morning,' he agreed, when we suggested going up on to the moors. 'But this afternoon, I've got to go to Newcastle by bus. I've a rehearsal.'

'By the way, how is the music going, Sebastian?' I asked, as we saddled up.

'Oh, it's OK,' he answered. 'If all goes well, I'll be with you in London in the summer.'

'And the orchestral concert you're giving?' I questioned. 'Where is it to be held and when?'

'It's to be in the Blackett Hall, Newcastle,' answered Sebastian proudly. 'On the Saturday after Christmas. I specially arranged it to be while you're here.' Then he struck an attitude and added in his most dramatic manner: 'All the world of music was gathered together in the Blackett Hall, Newcastle-upon-Tyne, to hear the young composer, Sebastian Scott, conduct his own *Woodland Symphony*. This is the first time this major work has been performed in this country. The first movement shows the influence of the composer's countryside upon his work – one can hear the northern wind blowing through his music. The second is a complete contrast in its equisitely gay and delicate broken chords and *arpeggios*, the personification of larch trees in spring; whilst the last movement works up, in a rising crescendo, to a terrific climax of crashing chords, making one think of the stormy winter wind as it shrills and trumpets through the bare branches of the northern forests. Gradually the storm subsides, the snow begins to fall softly, and a winter moon sails out over the tree-tops . . .'

'Gosh Sebastion – it sounds wonderful!' I exclaimed. 'I can hardly wait until next week! I like the idea of the trees in all their moods.'

'I hope the critics will do likewise,' said Sebastian solemnly, making me a little mock bow.

I stared at him thoughtfully. He hadn't changed a bit since last September – not outwardly, anyway. He had never been what you might call good-looking, but he had an interesting face with a high-bridged, sensitive nose, deeply set blue eyes, so dark that they looked almost black, and a crooked mouth. His black hair was cropped very short, and it fairly shone and bristled with life. Yes, that was what struck you about Sebastian – he was so very much alive. From the crown of his black head to the soles of his restless feet, tapping out an imaginary tune on the stable floor, he was full of energy. Looking at his tense young face, I knew that this concert in a tiny unknown hall somewhere in one of the poorest parts of Newcastle, meant just as much to Sebastian as it would to me if I were going to dance the Lilac Fairy on Covent Garden stage.

'Will there be many there – critics, I mean?' Caroline was asking.

'Well, I'm hoping that Billy Wilson of the *Northumbrian News* will turn up,' answered Sebastian. 'He sort of promised me he would.'

'Billy Wilson?' repeated Fiona. She had turned her back on us, and was standing looking out of the stable door, but now she turned round. 'You mean that awful little man who runs the ghastly women's page in *Northumbrian News* – "Aunt Emily's Whispers", or something?'

' "Aunt Emily's Whiskers"?' I echoed in astonishment.

'*Whispers*, girl; *whispers*!' corrected Sebastian solemnly, while Caroline burst into a gale of laughter. 'And let me tell you, Fiona, that just because a fellow has to earn his daily bread by catering for a lot of neurotic women, isn't to say he doesn't know anything about music. Matter of fact, Billy Wilson is dead keen on it; he's thinking seriously of joining my Scott Musical Society.'

'Oh, I see,' said Fiona sweetly, leading Melisande, her pony, out of the stable and springing into the saddle. 'Perhaps that explains why he'll be at the concert.'

Before Sebastian had time to make a suitable retort she was away over the field and out of earshot.

We had a glorious ride on the moors that stretched away on every side round Bracken Hall. Fiona joined us on our way back. She seemed as if she didn't really want to be with us, yet didn't want us to go off on our own. Perhaps she was afraid of missing something. The keen air made us so hungry that we couldn't wait for lunch, so we all trooped into the kitchen, and ate home-made scones covered with yellow country butter.

'And here's your milk, Miss Veronica,' said Trixie, putting a glass of it down on the table. 'Your Aunt June's orders! She says you're paler than ever, and indeed you are. It's all those late nights, I shouldn't wonder, and parties and that!'

In vain I tried to explain to Trixie that I didn't have any late nights; that life at the Sadler's Wells Ballet School was almost monastic in its simplicity – in other words, we did nothing but work, work, work, until at night we were too tired to do anything but go to bed. She only looked at me unbelievingly.

'Well, I *am* surprised, Miss Veronica. I always thought the stage was as gay as gay. I've no doubt you squeeze in a few parties somehow.'

'No, Trixie – really I don't,' I assured her. 'You see, I'm not actually on the stage yet, and even if I were—' I stopped trying to explain to Trixie that a ballet dancer – even a famous one – has to keep on exercising all the time; has to lead such a hightly specialized and artificial life that she has no time for the sort of pleasures ordinary people enjoy.

'Oh, look!' I cried, changing the subject, as a beautiful blue Persian cat strolled into the kitchen. 'There's Cleopatra! Oh, she's forgotten me, the old hag!'

Both Sebastian and Caroline began to laugh.

'*That's* not Cleo,' Caroline said. 'That's Ptolemy, Cleo's kitten. You remember – she had four of them just before you went back to London. Well, we got homes for three of them, but we just couldn't bear to part with Ptolemy; he's so beautifully dignified!'

I stared at Ptolemy in amazement. It seemed quite impossible to believe that the tiny kitten I'd played with last autumn could have grown into this beautiful cat in so short a time.

We stayed in the kitchen for a long while. I always think that the kitchen is the nicest room in the house – especially if it's a big country house. The kitchen at Bracken Hall was lovely; it had a red tiled floor, and an oak dresser with masses of deep blue willow-pattern china upon it. There was a long table, scrubbed to gleaming whiteness with silver sand, and a deep window-seat with red-and-white gingham cushions on it. Fiona didn't stay long, though. I think she imagined that sitting in the kitchen lowered her dignity! She said she'd go and 'tidy for lunch'.

'And I suppose we ought at least to wash our hands,' Caroline said with a sigh.

We trekked into the little cloakroom in the hall, and washed. I stole into the lounge, because I hadn't been in there yet. It was just the same as I remembered it. There was a huge oval posey bowl full of scarlet geraniums on the table between the long french windows, and another of yellow jasmine on the top of the grand piano. Opposite the jasmine was a photograph of Fiona in a silver frame, a photograph I hadn't seen before. She was wearing the new party frock that Caroline had told me about in her letter, and the photographer had got the light shining through her hair so that it looked like a halo. There was a smile hovering round her lips, and I was just thinking how beautiful she was when a voice behind me said:

'Self admiration society, what! Fiona thinking how devastating Fiona is!'

'Oh, Sebastian! What a fright you gave me!' I exclaimed. 'Why will you steal behind people like that'

'Sorry!' he apologized. Then he seated himself at the piano, after first turning the photograph so that its back was towards him, and began to play a gay, Hungarian tune. Of course, I couldn't resist it, and when Caroline and Fiona came in to see what was happening, they beheld me, skirts swirling, heels clicking, dancing the Czardas.

'That would be a lovely thing to do for Lady Blantosh's concert,' said Caroline. 'The people would adore it!'

'I haven't got a dress,' I objected. 'I've only my classical *tutu* with me, and I couldn't possibly dance a Czardas in *that*!'

'I've got a Hungarian skirt that I wore at a fancy-dress party,' Caroline said. 'And Fiona's got a lovely peasant blouse that Aunt Judith sent her from Czechoslovakia. It's got wide, embroidered sleeves.'

'It's not clean,' declared Fiona promptly. 'The last time I wore it I got jam on it.'

'Lie not, fair lady!' said Sebastian softly.

'How dare you! I'm not lying!'

'Aren't you? Well, let's go and find that blouse right now, and when you show me the jam on it, I'll believe you're telling the truth.'

'I shall do no such thing!' flashed Fiona. 'I don't allow boys to go messing about with my clothes. Anyway, it's gone to the laundry.'

'Oh, never mind,' put in Caroline. 'I've got a blouse you can wear, Veronica. It hasn't got embroidered sleeves, but it's a peasant blouse all right.'

'And I'll play for you,' Sebastian volunteered. 'That is, I will if you want me to.'

'Of *course* I want you to,' I said. 'I don't think there's a record of that thing, anyway. So if you don't play for me I can't dance.'

I said the words jokingly, never dreaming that before long they'd be anything but a joke.

Chapter 13

Northumbrian Interlude

THE holidays simply flew. The next day was Sunday, and I'm afraid that none of us went to church – at least, none of us except Fiona. As Sebastian said, we went to church most Sundays, so we could be excused for taking just one day off.

'It'll be a relief,' he added, 'not to have to listen to old Robson singing flat!'

As I have said, when we told Fiona of our proposed ride over to Broomyhough, she said she was going to church.

Sebastian made a face.

'Oh, yes, of course!' he remarked. 'I forgot you'd want to wear your new hat.'

'I want to do no such thing!' declared Fiona hotly. 'I don't go to church just to wear a new hat.'

'Don't you?' said Sebastian, goading her. 'It's a queer thing, Fiona, but whenever you go to church you happen to be wearing something new you want to show off. I've noticed it most particularly.'

'You've got a horrible mind,' stated Fiona.

'Granted,' Sebastian retorted imperturbably. 'Horrible, but discerning. By the way, that little tick, Ian Frazer, will be home for the holidays this weekend, and I shouldn't wonder if he wasn't at church too. I suppose that couldn't be the reason why you're so keen on going?'

Sebastian had at last achieved his goal. Fiona blushed hotly.

'You are a beast!' she flashed. 'And there's one thing about Ian – he wouldn't go about on Sunday dressed like you are, in a sweater all over leather patches, and a pair of riding-breeches that look as if Perkins has been cleaning the car with them!'

'I'm going riding, my good girl!' retorted Sebastian, tapping his riding-boot with his crop. 'I don't go riding in a white tie and tails! I don't go riding just to show off my clothes – like some people do!'

Sebastian had got in the last word, as so often happened. It was a well-known fact that Fiona only rode when she could look nice.

We sat in the lounge while Trixie put up our sandwiches, and we talked a hundred to the dozen. We discussed the exact locality of Broomyhough, Caroline's domestic-science career, and, last but not least, Sebastian's concert. Eventually Trixie arrived with an enormous mountain of food, all done up in separate packages so that we could share them out between us, and so divide the load ... We stowed away the packages in our rucksacks, wound woolly scarves round our necks because there was a cold wind blowing from the north-east, and after this we were ready for our adventure.

'Come on, you lot! Let's be off!' yelled Sebastian, picking up his string gloves from the table. 'I hope you enjoy the vicar's sermon, Fiona, and that there aren't too many things – or people – to distract your attention! And, by the way, it looks like rain or snow; you'd better take an umbrella to protect the new hat.'

'*I haven't got a new hat!*' Fiona yelled, and really I couldn't help feeling sorry for her – Sebastian was too bad with his teasing.

I loved that ride across the moors. Except for an occasional shepherd and his dog at an outlying farm, we didn't meet a soul, unless you could count curlews and rabbits and an occasional family of partridges solemnly taking a walk in the heather. Once we saw an old dog-fox standing motionless on a heathery crag, sniffing the wind. As we approached, he loped off and disappeared into the bracken like a shadow.

We crossed the main Newcastle–Jedburgh road, northwest of Otterburn, and then set off again across the open moorland, Sebastian leading us by ways known only to himself. We skirted dangerous patches of bog, crossed deep ravines that cut great gashes in the hills, trotted along sheep-tracks.

We stopped at eleven o'clock to have lunch and to rest the ponies, and I can tell you we made short work of the food Trixie had given us! Slices of ham-and-egg pie, sandwiches, slabs of fruit cake – all vanished as if we had never had a square meal in our lives!

'We simply must save something for later on,' Sebastian said firmly. 'Look here – let's keep the granny-loaf, and the rice cake, and some of the biscuits.'

'What about something to drink?' asked Caroline. 'We've finished off every spot of coffee.'

'We can try to get some tea or milk at a farm. I know the people at Corbyrigg; they'll give us something to drink like a shot, if we call there. They'll probably come up trumps and trot out a few eatables as well – when they see how little we've got left.'

'Oh, Sebastian!' I expostulated. 'How can you! Why, we've got *masses* left.'

'You wait till you've ridden to Broomyhough and back,' quoth Sebastian. 'You won't call it masses then!'

I must admit, here and now, that he was quite right. It's funny how, when you've just finished a meal, you think you can never be hungry again, but in an hour or two's time you feel you can eat a house!

It was one o'clock when we crossed the River Coquet above Alwynton, and then we had only a few more miles to go, and we'd be at our destination. The country was getting very wild and beautiful. The Coquet left off being a river and became a mountain stream, with waterfalls, and shallows, and a stony bank. To the north brooded Cheviot, her round brow capped with snow. The air was so cold that when you took a gulp of it, it was like drinking iced lemonade!

We dismounted to rest the ponies, and sat down with our backs against a drystone wall which sheltered us from the wind. Caroline produced a packet of clear gums, and we sat chewing them for quite a long time without speaking.

'Here's somebody on horseback,' said Sebastian suddenly. 'Let's ask him exactly where Broomyhough is, and the quickest way to get there. My knowledge of the country gives out hereabouts.'

The newcomer was mounted on what Sebastian called a heavy hunter. At first we thought he was a farmer, but when he got near enough to hail we saw that, although he wore breeches and a deerstalker, he had on a round collar.

'Parson,' whispered Sebastian. 'Golly! He looks a tough customer!'

The clergyman was a middle-aged man with two-coloured hair, and a fair skin that had been tanned to a ruddy brown by the winter winds. He had very blue eyes that looked like a sailor's do – as if he were used to looking long distances. He seemed very much at home on his big horse.

'Hullo!' yelled Sebastian. 'Please, could you tell us how to get to Broomyhough?'

The stranger reined in his mount, and sat smiling down at us. His splendid white teeth shone in his bronzed face.

'Broomyhough? Just a mile or so to the west. If you keep to the right of the crags' – he motioned to an outcrop of black rocks in the distance – 'and ride straight on, you'll see it in front of you. You'll want to be at the farm, I suppose?'

'No,' said Sebastian. 'We want a Mrs Mason. She lives at one of the cottages.'

'Granny Mason, who lives with young Adam Herdman?' said the parson. 'Oh, Granny's in great fettle, as they say round here! I saw her as I passed that way not half an hour ago; she's got her granddaughter home from London.'

'Yes, we know,' I put in eagerly. 'Stella's a great friend of mine.'

'Nice girl, Stella Mason,' volunteered the parson. 'Nice fellow she's got engaged to, as well.'

I gasped.

'Engaged? Stella engaged?' I stammered at length. 'You mean – engaged to be married?'

'Why, yes,' laughed the parson. 'This very day – to someone she knew in London – an artist chap.'

'*Jonathan!*' I shrieked. 'Gosh! How wonderful! I never *thought* of Jonathan!'

'They came to me this morning, early, to put the banns in,' went on the parson. 'Good-looking pair.' Then he sighed. 'I fear it'll be a blow to young Adam Herdman; always had an eye for Stella, had Adam.'

'Adam Herdman?' I questioned.

'Adam is shepherd to Mr Strong of Broomyhough,' explained the stranger. 'That's the big farm,' he added for our benefit, although we knew it already. Then he went on, almost to himself. 'Of course, you can understand Stella's point of view. A full-blown baronet is a different proposition altogether to a poor hill shepherd, and you can't blame her. All the same, it will be a blow to Adam.'

But my thoughts weren't for Adam Herdman, whoever he might be. They were all for the astonishing news about Jonathan – Jonathan, engaged to Stella; Jonathan, the poor artist, living in Mrs Crapper's dingy apartment house; Jonathan, whom our new friend was calling a full-blown baronet. It just didn't seem sense!

'*What* did you say he was?' I demanded when I had got my breath. 'You didn't really say he was a – a *baronet*, did you?'

'Exactly,' laughed the clergyman. 'That's what I said. Didn't you know? His father was Sir William Craymore, and then Mr Jonathan quarrelled with the old man, and went off to London to paint. He used the name of Rosenbaum because it belonged to a great friend of his who was killed in the war. Well, just a year ago, the old man died, and young Mr Jonathan came into the title.'

'Then Jonathan is really Sir Jonathan Craymore?' I said,

feeling more and more astonished. 'And, in that case, Stella will be Lady Craymore.'

The parson nodded his head.

'That's right. The family seat is at Ravenskirk, on the Border.' He jerked his head northwards. 'It's a fine old hall.'

'I wonder if they'll live there?' I said thoughtfully. 'Somehow, I just can't imagine Stella as Lady of the Manor, and president of the Women's Institute, and all that – she's much too shy. And I simply can't think of Jonathan as Squire either. Why, he'd hate hunting and shooting and all the rest of it. Jonathan wouldn't kill a fly!'

'I expect they won't live there,' smiled our new acquaintance. 'Or at least, not all the time. I understand an agent is looking after the place.'

'And this Adam Herdman you were talking about?' I questioned. 'Does he live with Stella's granny? How funny Stella never mentioned him.'

'I expect she was shy,' said the parson, 'seeing she knew how Adam thought about her. Old Granny Mason has lived in that cottage for close on sixty years. She went to it as a bride when she married Andrew Mason, who was shepherd to the Strongs. She was only twenty then. Andrew died a year or so ago in the Great Storm. Both Adam's brothers died with him. They were lost in the hills in a blizzard, looking for sheep. That was the 1947 storm – the biggest in living memory. More than five hundred sheep perished on the moors here.'

'Poor things – were they buried?' I asked.

'Some of them. Ordinarily, of course, sheep can lie buried for quite a long time and emerge hale and hearty, but this particular storm was just one long succession of blizzards, and, at the end, the sheep were so exhausted they just lay down and died. Those that didn't actually die in the snow, died afterwards when they gave birth to their lambs. It was a bad business altogether.'

'It must have been awful,' I said, looking round at the huge, rounded hills, and endless expanse of wild moorland. 'I can just imagine this place deep in snow. Looking for sheep would be like looking for needles in a haystack!'

'Well, Mr— I'm afraid we don't know your name,' put in Sebastian, getting up and tightening Warrior's girths. 'We shall have to be moving off, or we shan't be home before dark. We've enjoyed the "crack".'

The parson smiled.

'I've enjoyed it myself,' he answered. 'My name's Robson, by the way.'

'Goodbye, Mr Robson!' we chorused. Then we swung ourselves on to our ponies' backs, and rode off towards the crags, and he rode away in the opposite direction.

When we had rounded the corner of the rocks, we could see below us the big farmsteading of Broomyhough, and the one or two small cottages clustered round it like chickens round a hen. The friendly sounds of a dog barking and a cow lowing in a byre reached our ears, and, far up on a hillside above the farm, we could see the figure of a man with a sheepdog at his heels. His tiny figure served to accentuate the spaciousness of the rolling landscape.

The farm was situated on the north bank of the Coquet, so that it stood with its broad front facing south. A small plantation of stunted fir trees sheltered the house from the north winds. To the east, where the stream curved, we could see that the valley narrowed to a mere gash in the hills, and a glint of silver betrayed the presence of a waterfall.

'It will be glorious in the summer,' I said, half to myself. In my imagination I saw the bare, brown hills standing deep in bracken and purple heather, the larks singing in the blue air, the curlews wheeling.

'Come on – what are you stopping for?' said Sebastian impatiently, urging Warrior into a canter. 'We haven't any time to waste, you know, if we're to be home by dark. We shall have to ride back an awful lot quicker than we came, I can tell you!'

We had just crossed the stream by a tiny stone bridge and were trying to decide which cottage was the one we were looking for, when a young man appeared round the corner of the wall surrounding the farm. He had a stout stick in one hand and carried a bucket of water in the other.

'Good morning,' he said politely. 'It is a nice day for a ride.' He spoke in a slow, hesitating voice that sounded as if he wasn't used to talking to many people. Incidentally, I noticed that he was a handsome stripling of about twenty, tall and sunburnt, with hair bleached almost white, and a lean, tanned face. His eyes were very blue, and had the same far-away expression in them that we had noticed in the clergyman's. Altogether, he reminded me of a picture of 'The Boy David' in one of Caroline's Bible story-books.

'Look here,' said Sebastian, reining in Warrior. 'You don't happen by any chance to be Adam Herdman, do you?'

'That is my name,' answered the young shepherd with a smile. 'You will be wanting Mr Strong of Broomyhough, maybe?' He nodded over his shoulder at the big farm behind its wall.

'Oh, no,' said Sebastian. 'It's you we want. At least, it's the cottage where you live. We've come to see Mrs Mason. Veronica, here, is a great friend of her granddaughter, Stella.'

A cloud passed over the young man's face. He bent down and flicked a bit of wool from off his riding-breeches.

'This is where Mrs Mason lives,' he told us, indicating the cottage, 'but you will not find Stella here. She has become hand-fasted this day to a London gentleman, and they are gone to Ravenskirk, where he lives.'

'Oh, I see,' I said with a sigh of disppointment. 'Well, we'll just call and see her granny, now we're here. We've come from Bracken,' I added.

'Bracken? That is a very long way in the wintertime,' said the young man gravely. 'You must have something to eat – it will be late before you get home. There is a stable where you can put your horses. If you will please go in, I shall be back shortly. You can tie up your ponies here.' He indicated some hooks on the wall by the side of the door. 'I will see to them for you.'

He pushed open the door a little wider for us, set down the brimming bucket on the stone slab outside, and disappeared in the direction of the farm. He was certainly one of the most courteous and softly spoken young men we had ever met.

'I say,' said Sebastian, knocking on the door with the butt end of his riding-crop, 'we can't just walk in, can we? She might be having a bath, or anything!'

But there was no answer to his knock, and finally we stepped inside the door and looked around us. We were in a small kitchen in which everything that could possibly shine, shone. Even the patterned canvas on the floor reflected the simple furniture, so that the effect was rather like that of a lake, with the 'clipping' mats floating in it like islands. There was a bright fire in the hearth, with a steel fender in front of it, and a glittering array of fire-irons at either side. The knob of the oven door and the hinges shone and winked, and on the tiny dresser, brass plates and jugs gave back the light of the one small window. On the cottage piano, which had a front of pleated green silk and two brass candlesticks on either side of the music-rest, stood an array of photographs. They were all of Stella – Stella as a little girl, playing with a puppy; Stella obviously going to school for the first time, her books under her arm, and her smile no less bright for the fact that two of her front teeth were missing! There were several pictures of Stella in her ballet dress, and very strange it looked in this wild and primitive place to see her posed *en pointe* in her classic *tutu* and severely dressed hair.

There were several pictures on the walls of the room.

' "The Stag At Bay",' I read out, glancing at the one nearest me. 'Ugh! I'd hate always to have to be looking at that! But perhaps you get used to it, and don't notice it.'

There was another picture called 'The Trysting Place', which showed a girl in a very short-waisted dress, that made

110

her look at least seven feet tall, leaning against a tree in a very dejected attitude.

'Fellow hasn't turned up, obviously!' said Sebastian, looking over my shoulder.

For about five minutes we stood in that kitchen, wondering what to do, and where Stella's granny could have got to. Then there was the sound of a door opening somewhere at the back of the cottage, and a little old lady came into the room. She was very frail, and very, very old, but she had Stella's blue eyes, and Stella's shy smile. In her hands she was carrying two brown eggs which she placed carefully on the white-scrubbed table. Then she looked at us inquiringly.

When we had explained who we were, and what we had come for, Stella's grandmother took us to her heart. Nothing was too much trouble for the friends of her darling. She filled the kettle in a trice, and set it on the reddest part of the fire; then she covered the table with a snowy cloth, and blue-and-white willow-patterned china, and in a very short time we were sitting down to a real farmhouse tea of buttered scones and jam, a large home-made fruit cake, thick yellow cream, and cups of hot, strong tea.

Not until we had finished our meal did Stella's grandmother broach the subject which filled all our minds.

'You said you had met Adam?' she questioned. 'Did he tell you about the young man who came here for Stella?'

'Oh, yes,' I said. 'But we knew before that. Mr Robson – a clergyman we met on the road – told us all about it.'

Old Granny Mason looked from one to another of us anxiously.

'Tell me about him,' she said nervously. 'Is he a good young man, like Adam here? I've always heard that artists are such a strange sort of people – not like ordinary folk.'

'Yes,' I said thoughtfully. 'Yes, you're right – Jonathan isn't a bit ordinary. For one thing, he's so simple in his ways. He's so tall and broad, but, although he's immensely strong, he's ever so gentle. He's only twenty-six, you know, but you'd

111

think he was lots older. He'll look after Stella like a mother, and that's what Stella needs. They'll be so happy – why, Mrs Mason, what's the matter?' – for Stella's grandmother had put her head down on the edge of the table, much to Sebastian's discomfort, and was crying.

'It's all right, dearies,' she sobbed. 'I'm just relieved, that's all. You've taken a load off my mind. I was so afraid – you see, him being a baronet, and my little Stella—'

'We had no idea he was a baronet ourselves until this afternoon,' I volunteered. 'He never told us.'

'He never told anybody,' said Mrs Mason. 'Not even Stella. When old Sir William died, over a year ago, and Mr Jonathan became *Sir* Jonathan, he said he never thought to mention it.'

'Well!' I exclaimed. 'How exactly like Jonathan! And isn't it queer to think of Stella being Lady Rosenbaum – I mean, Lady Craymore, of course. I just *can't* get it into my head that Jonathan is Jonathan Craymore. and not Rosenbaum. It will be funny to hear Stella called Lady Craymore!'

'It will indeed!' said Granny Mason with a sigh. And whether it was a sigh of pleasure, relief, or just plain awe, I don't know!

We had pushed back our chairs and were preparing to go, when young Adam Herdman came in.

'Yes – it is time that you go home,' he said. 'Do not think that we want to be rid of you, but it is a long way to Bracken, and it is blowing up for snow. Already the storm has begun in the valley.' He nodded towards the east. 'Broomyhough has just come back from Bellingham, and he says it is inches deep down there already. Mistress Strong was anxious when she heard about you. She asked me to ask you if you will not stay the night over.'

'Good Lord, no!' exclaimed Sebastian. 'We must get back – I've got a rehearsal of my Music Society tomorrow.'

'It's most awfully kind of Mrs Strong, all the same,' I said. 'Please thank her for us, won't you, Mr—'

'Just Adam,' said the young man with a smile. 'Well, if you will not stay, you must be going quickly. It is not good for you to be caught in a snowstorm on these hills. It is all very well for me – I was born and bred here—'

'So was I,' Sebastian broke in indignantly. 'I should like to see the snowstorm that would get the better of me!'

'I was thinking, really, of the young ladies,' said the young shepherd, looking down at us.

'Well, Caroline's Northumbrian born and bred, too,' answered Sebastian. 'But perhaps you're right about Veronica. Veronica's a Londoner; she's nesh—'

'I like that!' I exclaimed. 'I'm not nesh at all – whatever it means. I'm pretty sure it's something horrid! And I'm not a Londoner. My mother was Northumbrian, so I'm half and half.'

'You *seem* like a Londoner,' insisted Sebastian. 'At least, you do since you've come back. But let's not argue about it. Adam's right, and we should be getting away. It's blowing up for snow and no mistake!'

It was a quarter past two when we left the cottage at Broomy-hough and started on our long ride home.

'Your Stella seems to be a bit of a lad!' remarked Sebastian, as we left the cottage behind and set off across the open moor.

'What do you mean?' I demanded indignantly.

'Well, it seems to me she's got two strings to her bow – this Jonathan chap, and young Adam Herdman. He's obviously three sheets in the wind, or however you describe people in love.'

'Stella can't help that,' I declared. 'It's not her fault if men fall in love with her. I think it's beastly of you, Sebastian, to call her names. Why, everyone loves Stella; you would yourself if you knew her.'

'Not me!' declared Sebastian. 'I'm in love already.'

'Yes – with yourself!' I retorted.

'What a noise you two make,' put in Caroline. 'If it wasn't for you, there wouldn't be another sound.'

We reined in our ponies and listened, and it was quite true. There was perfect and unbroken silence. There wasn't even the chirp of a bird, or the bleat of a sheep. There was something unearthly about it – as if the world were under a spell.

'London is like a dream,' I said as we went on again. 'When you think of all those people at this very moment fighting for buses and trains, being carried up and down in escalators and lifts; all those cars grinding along in endless procession – well, it just seems like another world. Yet, when I'm in London, Northumberland seems like a dream. It's queer, isn't it?'

As we rode onwards, we looked back over our shoulders, but we could no longer see Cheviot. A fine veil had fallen between us and the mountain.

'It's snowing up there,' said Sebastian with a note of anxiety in his voice. 'Come on, you lot! We must ride like Jehu!'

Chapter 14

Caught in the Snow

BUT though we rode like Jehu, or like the very wind itself, the storm gained upon us. Perhaps it was because we were riding eastwards, and the storm seemed to be blowing up from that quarter. Very soon the ground was several inches thick with fine snow, and the tufts of heather and coarse grass began to look like fat white cushions. Drifts of snow crept up the dry-stone walls and along the dykes, completely changing the face of the landscape.

It was then that I understood how truly Sebastian had spoken when he'd told Adam Herdman he was Northumbrian born and bred. He led us unerringly across the white wastes towards the Coquet, crossing the stream at the exact spot where we had crossed it that morning, and then onwards over the darkening moorland towards the distant Otterburn–Jedburgh road.

'I don't now how on earth you find your way,' I said in admiration after we had ridden for a long time without speaking. 'It all looks exactly the same to me!'

'Oh, I can tell where I am by the burns,' said Sebastian. 'They stay the same for ages, even in the snow. I know the look of most of them. Then there are the rocks. That outcrop over there, for instance – I know we must keep well to the south of that.'

'What would happen if we didn't?' I asked him.

'Bog,' answered Sebastian concisely. 'Not that it would matter just now, because it'll be frozen over, but it would be out of our course, and we don't want to be any longer getting home than we can help.'

'N-no, we d-don't,' I said with a shiver. Already my feet

were numb, and my face felt as if it were covered with a mask of ice.

'Here – catch!' yelled Sebastian. 'I said you were nesh!' He unwound his woollen scarf from round his neck and tossed it over to me. 'Now don't argue – put it on!'

I put it on meekly, glad of its extra warmth.

We rode on doggedly, Caroline on one side of me, Sebastian on the other. Icicles hung from the ponies' eyelashes, and a great dome of snow hid Arabesque's well-known dish-face from me. Hour after hour we rode, only stopping for a few minutes to eat the rest of our food, and give the ponies a breather. Although I had spent a winter with my cousin before I had gone back to London, it had been an abnormally mild one, and we had had very little snow. Now I learned for the first time what a real blizzard on the Northumbrian moors is like. The fine snow blew up round us in hissing, misty clouds, stinging our faces as if it were made of particles of steel, or sharp glass. The high parts of the moor had blown clear, but the hollows were filled with great drifts, and we had to pick our way round them. They were like lakes of snow, growing deeper every moment. All around us was a desolate waste of snow, with not a village or a habitation of any sort within sight. There wasn't even a sheep-stell. Nothing but snow beneath us, and curling skies above us, as far as the eye could see. It was savage and awe-inspiring, and if it hadn't been for Sebastian and Caroline riding steadily along beside me, seemingly quite unmoved by any feeling of terror, I'd have been scared to death. Long afterwards Sebastian told me that he hadn't been quite as unmoved as he had seemed during that long ride. He'd begun to wonder whether we would ever be able to find our way home, not because of the snow, but because of the early winter twilight which was closing down upon us with terrifying swiftness. To be caught on a lonely Northumbrian moor at night in a blizzard would be almost certain death. Fortunately, I didn't know this. I had implicit faith in Sebastian. I knew he would lead us home safely.

'I thought you said there was a farm hereabouts by the name of Corbyrigg?' said Caroline, breaking the long silence. 'You talked about getting some tea there on our way back.'

'We seem to have missed it somehow,' answered Sebastian. 'I think we've come a bit far north.'

We had crossed the Otterburn–Jedburgh road long ago, and were now on the last long stretch of moor that led to home. It was getting dark and our ponies were beginning to stumble.

Suddenly Sebastian gave a great shout.

'Gosh, Caroline! Do you see what this is? This means we're OK.'

Before us rose a queer old stone building, something like a house, only it didn't seem to have any windows in the bottom part of it. It had a heavy iron-studded door and a flight of worn, stone steps leading to the top floor.

'It's the old peel-house above Garside!' said Caroline with a gasp of relief. 'Thank goodness! We aren't far from home now. Golly! I was beginning to think we were well and truly lost.'

'So was I,' admitted Sebastian. 'But I knew we *ought* to come to this place sooner or later, if we were where I thought we were.'

'What about staying here for the night?' suggested Caroline. 'It's quite a cosy place up top.'

But Sebastian shook his head.

'No,' he said. 'They'll dig us out at the Hall in a day or two, but up here we'd probably be snowed up for weeks, and there's my concert on Saturday – besides the rehearsals.'

I couldn't help reflecting that I wasn't the only person to have a one-way mind. Sebastian ran me very close.

We skirted the queer old building and rode off to the right, passing by a mountain tarn on our way. Its waters were dark and infinitely lonely, and I couldn't help giving a shudder as I looked at it. On a hot summer's day, with the larks overhead, and the bees in the heather on its banks, its grey waters ruffled by waterfowl, it would be a pleasant enough place, no doubt,

117

but just now, seen through a veil of snow, it looked a spot of the utmost desolation. An uncanny, haunted place! I wasn't sorry to turn my back on it, I can tell you!

We were riding now almost due south, and before long we struck a country road. I say 'road', but really it looked more like a railway cutting! The snow had blown into drifts that were as high as your head on the one side and tailed off into rivulets on the other. The strips of black road, seen in between, had the effect of railway sleepers. The snowy rivulets lying across our path were so regular that I began to feel sleepy, and as though I were mesmerized. My head drooped forward, and several times I found myself slipping over Arabesque's neck. Then, as though in a dream, I heard Sebastian say:

'Ah! This is what I've been looking for! The telephone kiosk on the Bracken road. We'll ring up and let them know we're OK.'

'Veronica's nearly asleep,' I heard Caroline answer.

'Wake her up, then!' came Sebastian's voice. 'For goodness' sake keep her awake while I phone.'

I heard him dismount, go into the box, shovelling away a drift of snow first with his foot, and begin to talk. I heard him say something about our whereabouts, and then: 'Ask Perkins to get out the shooting-brake – it can get through this stuff – and come and meet us. Oh, not for Caroline and me – we're OK. It's Veronica – she's just about all in! She's not like us; she's town bred!'

I was too tired even to be angry at his words. I slipped from Arabesque's back and lay down on the ground beside the telephone kiosk with a sigh of thankfulness. It was really quite cosy in the snow – soft – cosy—

Rudely I was pulled to my feet.

'Get up, Veronica! Get up, I say! ... Caroline, I *told* you not to let her go to sleep – oh, yes, you could!— Get up this very minute, Veronica! Don't you know it's dangerous to go to sleep in the snow.'

'Let me alone!' I begged. 'Really, I'm quite comfy here.'

Then the most astonishing thing happened. Sebastian raised his hand, and struck me a resounding slap on the cheek. It wasn't a light, playful blow either; it was a hard one, and it hurt. I was so surprised that my eyes flew wide open, and I leapt to my feet.

'How dare you!' I yelled in a fury. 'How dare you!'

Sebastian's blue eyes snapped fire.

'That's better! Now will you do as you're told, and come on? Up you get, and don't you go falling asleep again, or I shall do it even harder!'

On we rode, and after what seemed hours, though Sebastian said afterwards it was only about twenty minutes, we heard the welcome sound of a motor vehicle churning through the snow, its chains clinking and grinding. A few more seconds and the shooting-brake loomed out of the darkness, its headlights turning the snowy landscape into fairyland.

'Get Veronica inside,' Sebastian said to Perkins, who was driving the brake. 'You'd better go as well, Caroline, to look after her. I'll come on behind, and Arab and Gilly will follow if we unbridle them.'

Then came the question of turning the shooting-brake in the road. We decided that it was impossible, so Perkins reversed it to the cross-roads past which he'd come a few minutes before.

And so we arrived at Bracken Hall. The whole house turned out to welcome us – even Fiona. Trixie stood in the hall, surrounded by a perfect forest of hot-water bottles, warm blankets, and cups of steaming coffee. Really, it made us feel as if we were Arctic explorers who had been thought lost, but who had reached haven at last!

'Oh, Veronica,' said Sebastian, when I had recovered a bit and was trekking off for a hot bath, 'you know, when I hit you out there it was sheer necessity, don't you? I just *had* to do something drastic to wake you up, or you'd have been as dead as a door-nail before very long. You do understand, don't you?'

'Of course I do,' I assured him. 'It certainly *did* wake me up! As a matter of fact – I've been thinking – I believe you saved my life, Sebastian.'

'Oh, rot!' said Sebastian with a grin.

Chapter 15

A Northumbrian Christmas

APART from a little stiffness, I didn't suffer any ill-effects from my adventure, and as for Sebastian and Caroline, they seemed to take it all as a matter of course.

'Snowed up!' said Sebastian cheerfully when we met at breakfast next morning – he had stayed at Bracken Hall for the night – 'I thought we would be! Christmas Eve is the day after tomorrow, so it looks as if we'll be cut off from civilization for the Festive Season. Oh, well, it doesn't really matter. I shall only miss one rehearsal, and the turkey's in the larder! Fortunately, it arrived yesterday, before the snow started.'

'By the way,' put in Caroline, 'Mrs Strong of Broomyhough rang up last night, after we'd gone to bed, to find out if we'd arrived home safely. Wasn't it decent of her?'

'Jolly decent,' agreed Sebastian. 'These outlying people are miles ahead of the others when it comes to natural good manners. I've often noticed.'

After breakfast we climbed up into the attics to view the landscape. It was a lovely sight. The snow had stopped falling, and the sky was a beautiful duck-egg blue. All round the Hall the hills rose in glittering white tiers, while nearer at hand the fir trees stood like sentinels, each branch covered with its snowy burden. During the night the wind had blown the fine snow into fantastic shapes. Each bush had its spiral, each stone a shell of snow curving over its back, while snow hung in glistening scallops round the roof and over every window. There was an arbour of snow over the front porch. Just as we stared at it, fascinated, Perkins came round the corner of the house and demolished it with a long-handled shovel.

'He *would* go and do that!' exclaimed Sebastian, who had

no love for Perkins. 'Trust Perkins to spoil the artistic effect!'

'Oh, I expect Aunt June told him to do it,' I said.

From our lofty position we could see curls of smoke rising from farms and hamlets all over the snowy landscape, and it was queer to think that we were entirely cut off from them.

'Look!' exclaimed Sebastian, who had found a pair of binoculars and was gazing through them. 'You see those black specks – over there, by the village? They're the road-gang. They've started to cut us out already. Ahoy there!'

A faint shout answered his hail.

'Let me have the glasses,' I begged.

He passed them over to me, and immediately the specks changed into a little group of men, in their shirt-sleeves, shovelling the snow into great blocks and tossing them on to the sides of the road.

'Glasses, please!' said Caroline after a few minutes. 'It's maddening to have somebody looking through field-glasses, and exclaiming about things, and not being able to see them for yourself.'

'Sorry,' I laughed, and passed them over. 'How long will it take them to get to us, Sebastian?'

'Oh, they ought to be here by the day after tomorrow,' he answered. 'We should be cut out by Christmas Eve, provided there isn't another fall.'

But that night the wind rose, and it began to snow again, so that the track dug by the roadmen was blown in, and they had to start all over again.

'Never mind,' said Sebastian. 'We're entirely self-supporting here. We've food for months in the house – except meat, and we can always kill off the hens and chickens if we're starving – not to mention the pig! By the way, you lot, we must have a Christmas tree. How about getting one out of the wood? We could chop it down ourselves, and bring it back on a sledge.'

'Oh, yes – let's!' we said in chorus. 'That would be fun!'

We spent the rest of the day digging a track for ourselves

towards the nearest fir plantation. I couldn't help wondering what the people at Sadler's Wells would have thought if they'd seen me cutting out huge blocks of snow and heaving them over my shoulder! At intervals I took a scared look at my arms to see if the muscles were bulging, but no – all seemed to be well! I felt sure that everyone would approve of the pink colour that was creeping into my pale cheeks.

Perkins and the gardeners spent their time cutting a path out to the field, so that Aunt June could feed her hens, and another one round to the garage for Uncle John to get to his car. This seemed to me to be rather optimistic, because, even if Uncle John had been able to get his car out, he wouldn't have been able to go anywhere in it. However, I suppose he wanted to be ready to emerge the very moment the men got through from the village. As a matter of fact, as things turned out, I was to thank Uncle John for his forethought before many days were passed.

In the late afternoon we set off, armed with axe, sledge, and ropes, along the track we had made to bring home our Christmas tree. Sebastian cut it down and we all helped to drag it on to the sledge. When I say 'all', I don't include Fiona. She didn't like messing about in the snow, or cutting down trees. She stayed behind and helped Aunt June and Trixie with the flowers that Pilks had brought in from the hot-houses.

We deposited the Christmas tree in the hall, ready to be set up in a huge plant-pot, and went back to the garden for holly. We found, to our disgust, that the birds had eaten most of the berries, but Sebastian found one small tree that still had a lot on, so we piled our sledge high with branches of it.

'Mistletoe!' said Sebastian when we'd finished. 'There's some growing on that old apple tree in the kitchen garden. Come on you people!'

We trekked round to the kitchen garden, ploughing through the snow in our Wellington boots, and there, sure enough, Sebastian was right. The gnarled branches of the apple tree were covered with the pale-green leaves and waxen berries of the beautiful parasite. We picked a huge bunch and placed it carefully on top of the holly. Then we dragged the sledge round to the front door and unloaded our booty in the porch, so that we could carry it straight into the hall where the Christmas tree was to be placed and where most of our decorating was to be done.

'Make way for Santa Claus!' yelled Sebastian, striding into the hall, his arms full of greenery. He threw it down on the floor and then held aloft the bunch of mistletoe.

'Let me see,' he exclaimed, striking an attitude. 'What is this stuff for? Ah, yes – methinks I remember!'

Before I knew what he was about, he had held it over my head and kissed me under it.

'That's to make up for the horrid way I treated you yesterday, when we were out in the storm!' he declared.

'How did you treat her in a horrid way?' demanded Fiona curiously. She'd been standing in the shadows, arranging geraniums in a low rose bowl, and now she came forward. 'What do you mean?'

'Oh, I slapped her face, that's all,' said Sebastian offhandedly. He was never averse to shocking Fiona if he got the chance. 'Had to. Otherwise she'd have been like the maiden in Wordsworth's poem – Lucy somebody or other – who was lost in the snow. Dead as a haddock! I just had to wake her up.'

'So you slapped Veronica's face – how gentlemanly!' said Fiona sarcastically.

'As I say – it had to be done,' countered Sebastian. 'Better to be ungentlemanly than to have Veronica's death laid at my door! Never was particularly gentlemanly, as you may have noticed. Anyway, she's forgiven me – haven't you, Veronica?'

I couldn't help laughing. Fiona was so serious, and Sebastian so wicked, standing there deliberately baiting her.

'Of course I have,' I answered.

'Oh, well – if you don't *mind* being slapped,' said Fiona with a shrug. 'I shouldn't care for it myself, though.'

'No, you'd rather be as dead as a haddock!' said Sebastian. 'Queer tastes some people have, I must say!' He began to arrange the holly round the picture frames, singing at the same time:

> 'There was a young lady of Craddock
> Who'd rather be dead as a haddock.
> But alas, and alack!
> On her cheek a big smack
> Saved the life of our lady of Craddock!'

Fiona turned a little pink – she hated to be laughed at. Then she said curiously:

'I suppose you only kiss your friends under the mistletoe, Sebastian – not your cousins?'

'Cousins?' echoed Sebastian, pausing with a piece of mistletoe in his hand. 'Oh, you mean *you*? Rather not! No fun kissing cousins!'

'I suppose that goes for me, too?' put in Caroline.

'You? You're just a kid,' said Sebastian, turning and laughing down at her. 'No fun kissing babies!'

Of course, Caroline fell upon him in her wrath, whereupon he dropped the mistletoe, and fled up the shallow oak staircase and stood mocking us in the gallery above.

'Look out! You're scattering mistletoe berries all over the place!' yelled Caroline. 'Somebody will be slipping—'

She broke off suddenly. Her words had come true almost before they were out of her mouth. Trixie had come into the hall from the kitchen and had skidded on a rolling berry. She shot across the polished floor at the bottom of the stairs and collapsed against a suit of armour. I'm afraid we all began to laugh. Apart from the crash and clatter the armour made, Trixie's outraged expression was really funny.

'Trixie! Trixie!' came Sebastian's mocking voice from the gallery. 'I'm surprised – really I am – to find *you* of all people clasping Sir Humphrey O'Rourke, my illustrious ancestor,

125

round the middle! Really, Trixie! And from what I've heard, Sir Humphrey was more than a bit of a lad!'

'For shame, Master Sebastian!' said poor Trixie, extricating herself from the chilly embrace of the suit of armour that was reputed to have belonged to the old knight. 'It's your berries I've slipped on, and well you know it! Why you must drop everything down on the floor, I can't think. Such a lot of trouble untidy people make!' She went to the kitchen again, muttering about Sebastian and his untidiness; though, as a matter of fact, we all knew she adored him really.

Chapter 16

Christmas Day

WE all went to midnight mass on Christmas Eve, having persuaded Aunt June that it was really a good idea because it meant we wouldn't have to get up early to go to holy communion the next morning.

'Matter of fact, I've simply *got* to do some practising tomorrow morning. My concert is on Saturday – only two days off,' said Sebastian as we picked our way round the drifts by the aid of his flashlight.

'Yes, and Lady Blantosh's thing is on Friday – Boxing Day,' I said. 'I must practise as well. Why, I haven't decided yet what dances I'm going to do.'

'It's a good thing Lady Blantosh's concert is in the village hall here, and not at Blantosh,' remarked Caroline. 'Blantosh Castle is right up on the edge of the moors. I don't expect they'll be dug out there for ages. Poor old Lady Blantosh will have to walk down.'

'Do her good,' declared Sebastian, who had no love for Lady Blantosh, kind though she was. 'She's getting far too fat!'

By this time we had reached the church, and an unexpected and lovely sight greeted us as we walked up the little path to the porch. There happened to be a tall fir tree growing just outside the church door, and someone had had a brainwave and had hung its branches with fairylights, Canadian-fashion. When the wind blew, all the little coloured lights dipped and swung, and the effect was marvellous.

As I loooked at the dancing tree, I thought of Hans Andersen's Karen, dancing up to the church door in her red shoes, only to be turned back by the Angel of God with his stern face

*I thought of Hans Andersen's Karen, dancing up to the
church door in her red shoes*

and shining, white wings. Poor Karen, condemned to dance over highway and byway, in summer's heat and winter's cold – condemned to dance for ever, just because she was gay! It seemed a severe punishment!

'Come on, Veronica!' said Fiona's voice from in front of me. 'What on earth are you standing there for?'

'Oh, she's imagining things!' said Sebastian mockingly. 'Veronica often does, you know! What was it this time, Veronica – Giselle and her Wilis?'

I said nothing, but followed them into the church, past the carved coffin-lids that stood on end like sentinels just inside the porch, past the tomb where the Crusader, who was one of Sebastian's ancestors, lay, his dog at his feet, past the carved griffin whose outspread wings supported the Bible, and into the Scotts' family pew.

The church was decorated with holly and evergreens, and the altar was a mass of pink generaniums.

'Mummy did it this afternoon,' whispered Caroline, as we filed into our seats. 'Doesn't it look lovely?'

'Gorgeous,' I whispered back. 'I think the real candles in the candelabra are lovely, too. They give such a soft light – much nicer than electric ones.'

Walking back from the church in the snow at half past twelve at night was exciting. We made our way across the fields because the road was still blocked. Sometimes we came to huge drifts, and had to go a long way round, so it took us ages to get home. Or perhaps it was really because it was all so beautiful and unearthly, walking over the snow in the brilliant moonlight, that we didn't hurry!

When we reached the frozen lake, I lingered for a moment on its banks, and imagined myself dancing on it as Irma Foster had danced in *Les Patineurs*. The fronds of dead bracken, glittering under the frosty moon, reminded me of her white dress. I could almost hear the gentle, rippling music of the harp-strings, plucked by an unseen hand.

'Oh – lovely! Lovely!' I said half aloud.

'*Veronica!* Do hurry up!' came Fiona's impatient voice. 'Mummy will wonder where on earth we are!'

Sebastian came with us as far as the gate into the garden proper, and then went back to his cottage, whilst we trekked round to the kitchen and made coffee. After this, Caroline gave a great yawn and said that she was going to bed.

'Goodnight, everyone, and a Merry Christmas!'

'Merry Christmas!' Fiona and I said in reply. 'Just coming ourselves.'

Fiona and Caroline went to matins on Christmas morning, but I stayed at home and practised for Lady Blantosh's concert the next day. Sebastian joined us for lunch, and when that was over, he announced that he was going to spend the afternoon helping to dig out the road, together with a lot of other volunteers.

'Jolly self-sacrificing of me, I consider,' he stated, 'because it doesn't matter two hoots to me when the bally road is cut out. It's OK from the crossroads, and I can get a bus into Newcastle from there, so my rehearsal tomorrow afternoon is safe. Still, always the little gentleman, yours truly.'

'I thought you said yesterday—' began Fiona, but Sebastian cut her short with a lordly gesture.

'Quote me not dead yesterdays, woman!' he said. 'I live in the present. See you at tea, you lot! So long!'

With this he was gone, and we were left to our own devices. We spent most of the afternoon tying up the presents we had got for each other, and also the masses of small gifts that Aunt June had bought for the village children, who were coming to a party after dinner that night.

We tied the small gifts on the tree and arranged our own presents round the bottom because we were going to give them out earlier in the evening. When we had finished, it looked terribly exciting. We crawled round the tree on hands and knees, prodding and poking the intriguing parcels.

'I'll bet this one is a riding-crop,' said Caroline. 'Mummy

130

knew I'd broken mine at that gymkhana at Mintlaw last October.'

'And this will be a box of liquorice all-sorts,' I said. 'It's for me, and it's Trixie's writing. She knows how fond I am of them. But, of course, it *may* be a box of soap!'

'This one's got a gorgeous smell!' exclaimed Caroline. 'You can smell it right through the wrapping-paper! It's for you, Fiona; so it'll be that bath essence you wanted.'

'I wish you wouldn't keep on guessing!' grumbled Fiona. 'It spoils all the fun.'

Caroline got up with a sigh.

'Perhaps you're right,' she admitted. 'But it's an awful temptation. Oh, well – let's arrange the Christmas cards.'

'Mummy's and mine are in the lounge; we did them ages ago,' Fiona said loftily. 'You and Veronica had better put yours on the mantelshelf in here.'

Caroline had masses of lovely cards. Most of them had horses on them. Mine were chiefly ballet dancers, which was just as it should be. One was the exception, though. It was a private card from Lady Blantosh, and it was a view of Blantosh Castle, taken from the rose garden. Miss Martin, the principal of my Newcastle dancing school, had sent me a lovely card of Margot Fonteyn in *Swan Lake*, and I had a ballet calendar from Madame Viret. Sara, Stella, and several of my Northumbrian schoolfriends had remembered me, so I felt that I hadn't done too badly, all things considered. Jonathan and Mrs Crapper had both sent me exciting-looking parcels, but I had firmly put them round the Christmas tree with the others, to be opened later on.

'Let's go down to the bottom of the drive and see how the road-diggers are getting on,' I suggested, when we had got all the cards arranged to our liking. 'It's a lovely day overhead, as Trixie would say. The sun's as hot as midsummer!'

We found the road-gang within shouting distance of the gates. Sebastian was there, in shirt-sleeves, and working like a navvy. He was receiving a great deal of goodnatured chaff

131

because he was wearing a large pair of leather gloves to protect his hands. But teasing made no difference to Sebastian. He stuck to his gloves! I stared at him thoughtfully over the intervening wall of snow, and decided that no one could be blamed for not taking him or his ambition seriously. He went through life joking about everything, and it was rarely anyone saw the serious vein underlying his teasing manner. Few people – except perhaps his father and I – ever saw the serious side of Sebastian, or knew how terribly determined he was. I knew, though, that he would let nothing stand in the way of his ambition. He was a strange mixture, was Sebastian!

'View hullo!' he yelled half an hour later as the last block of snow was heaved on to the shoulder-high walls at the side of the road. 'We're out!'

The road-gang, composed of Uncle Adrian, Sebastian's father, the village schoolmaster, the doctor, and several people from houses nearby, leant on their shovels and mopped their heated brows. Bella MacIntosh, who looked after Sebastian and Uncle Adrian, brought a steaming pot of coffee, and handed it out through the window, together with a bevy of mugs. We drank our coffee, standing in the snowy road, and Sebastian perched himself astride a huge block of snow and made hissing noises through his teeth.

'Well, now for a real tea!' he announced, dismounting at length, and passing his cup through the window to the grinning Bella. 'That stuff has just whetted my appetite! I hope you've got something substantial, Bella? Ham and eggs, for choice!'

'You think of nothing but eating,' Fiona said scornfully.

'You ought to try doing a spot of work for a change,' retorted Sebastian. 'Improve your appetite! So long, folks! See you at dinner!'

So saying, he swung himself over the window-sill of the cottage and disappeared from our view. A moment later we heard the chords of the *Sonata Pathétique* coming out of the window and knew that we had seen the last of Sebastian for some time.

Usually Caroline and I had supper in the schoolroom, but of course tonight, being Christmas night, we had dinner with the grown-ups. We had it very early, because of the party to follow. Uncle Adrian was there, and the doctor and his wife, and, of course, Sebastian.

We all wore our prettiest dresses. Fiona had on the new long frock that she was wearing in the photograph. It was honey-coloured taffeta, and it exactly matched her hair. Caroline and I hadn't real evening frocks yet, so we just wore our best party dresses. Caroline's was her school prizegiving one, so of course it was white. Mine was a flowered summer dress that Aunt June had had made for me last year. Sebastian gave us all a shock by turning up in a real, grown-up dinner jacket. He told me on the quiet that he had got it especially for his concert on Saturday.

'The conductor must wear evening togs,' he declared.

'You look so grown up, I hardly dare talk to you!' I told him.

We had the usual Christmassy sort of things for dinner: turkey, plum pudding, and all the et ceteras. I told everyone that it was my second Christmas dinner, and of course they wanted to know how that could be, so I explained about Jonathan's pheasants, and Mrs Crapper's two puddings, and our festive dinner-table with its swan on a glass lake. Dr Ridley laughed and said it carried him back to his childhood. The housekeeper they'd had when his mother died had had a 'centrepiece' just like that!

While the grown-ups were having their coffee, we dashed into the hall to light the candles on the tree, so that it would burst upon them in a blaze of glory. We left the curtains undrawn, so that the lights were reflected in the long windows, and it looked exactly as if there were two trees, one at each end of the room.

When every candle was alight, and burning brightly, we dashed back to the dining-room and commanded the grown-ups to come quickly, because we didn't want the candles to burn quite away – we wanted to light them again later on for the village children, who were due at eight o'clock.

'And now for the presents,' Caroline said, when we'd extinguished the candles and switched on the lights. 'You give them out, Veronica, as you're kind of a visitor.'

'Yes – you, Veronica!' said everyone in chorus.

So I acted as Master of Presents, if you can call it that. I won't bother with a list of all the things everyone got, but will just tell you what my own presents were. Aunt June and Uncle John had given me a lovely twinset of Shetland wool, with a Fair Isle pattern on the jumper; Sebastian a photograph of Arabesque in a frame, so that I could put it in a place of honour on the mantlepiece at Heather Hill; Caroline a box of sweets that she'd made herself; Fiona a jar of bath salts that I happened to know someone had given her last Christmas but which weren't the kind she liked; lastly, Trixie's present *was* the box of liquorice all-sorts that we had felt when we'd been poking the parcels, and Mrs Crapper's was a jumper that she'd made herself. She'd got the pattern a bit mixed in places, but I knew that this was owing to her eyes not being what they were, and I loved it just as much as if it had been perfect. Oh, and I nearly forgot Jonathan and Stella. They'd sent me a joint present, and it was a pair of opera-glasses in a brocaded case. Jonathan had also put in a book, *Ivan Stcherbakof – by his Mother*, because he thought I hadn't read it.

'Hey, Veronica!' yelled Sebastian when I'd unwrapped the parcel. 'You can't start reading that now! There are loads of other things to give out!' He snatched the book out of my hands and put it under a cushion, which he then sat on. 'On with the dance! I mean the presents!'

As I looked at my beautiful gifts, my heart grew warm with gratitude to them all. I thought sadly of the inexpensive presents I'd had to give them, and hoped they wouldn't mind

134

them being cheap. I knew that Sebastian and Caroline wouldn't, but I wasn't sure about Fiona!

The children arrived promptly at eight, and Uncle Adrian appeared, dressed as Santa Claus, to give out the presents on the tree. Then we all played games, sang songs, and ate ice-cream that Aunt June had made in the fridge. After this, they all clamoured for me to dance. It appeared that a lot of the kids had been at Lady Blantosh's concert when I'd danced before, and they all wanted to see me again.

'Go on, Veronica!' begged Sebastian. 'I'll play for you if you like. What do you want? Something out of *The Sleeping Beauty*?'

'I can dance the Fairy of the Crystal Fountain,' I answered.

'OK. I can play that without the music,' said Sebastian.

He disappeared into the lounge and, without switching on the light, began to play. I dashed upstairs and put on my *tutu* and, in a few minutes I was back in the hall, no longer a schoolgirl in a much-washed party dress, but a real fairy. The village children thought so, anyway, if you could judge by their open mouths and wide eyes!

Uncle Adrian and Uncle John had rolled back the rugs, and the floor stretched before me, gleaming softly, inviting. The centre lights were turned off, leaving only the rose-shaded reading-lamps at each side of the fireplace.

Suddenly the hall, with its Christmas tree and its waiting people, seemed to fade away. I was in a beautiful garden. Tall cypress trees stood like sentinels, throwing their black shadows over the velvet lawns; the moon sailed free in a cloudless sky; in the shadowy depths of a magnolia tree a nightingale sang. In the middle of the garden was a marble statue – the dreaming figure of a girl. Rising and falling above her head rose a slender jet of water, glistening silver in the moonlight, and shining upon her white shoulders in pearly drops, to fall with musical splash into the marble basin at her feet.

And I was the fairy of this crystal fountain. I felt the glittering dewdrops caught in my hair, in the crisp folds of my dress. I felt the moonlight caress my upturned face like a lover. The music of the fountain spoke to my feet, and what could I do but listen to its call, and dance? So I rose *sur les pointes*, my arms *en attitude*.

I danced, and Sebastian accompanied me faultlessly as he always did. Although in my thoughts I was far away from the hall, yet I knew he was there at the piano. I'd have guessed instantly if someone else had taken his place. There was no one – no one at all who could accompany me like Sebastian!

At the end of my dance there was a burst of clapping. Sebastian said nothing, but his eyes told me what he really felt.

'Well, that's the first time I've seen you dance, young lady,' Uncle Adrian said, as I stood by the fire recovering my breath. 'And I can tell you that I shall look forward to seeing you again. It was a great pleasure to watch you – you were very beautiful. I had no idea you could dance like that.'

'Thank you,' I said with a smile. 'It's most awfully nice of you to say so.'

After the village children had gone home, I stole back to the deserted hall where the Christmas tree stood. One or two of its candles were still alight, and the log fire burned low in the grate. I went over to the uncurtained windows and looked out at the snowy garden and the white hills beyond.

'Beautiful, isn't it?' said a voice close behind me.

I jumped.

'Oh, Sebastian! What a fright you gave me! Do take care – you'll crush my *tutu*!'

He drew back a little.

'Sorry! I forgot you still had that stupid thing on. You don't think about anything but your dancing, do you Veronica? You don't think anything is as important as your dancing?'

'No, of course not,' I said in surprise. 'What a funny thing to say! No, of course, nothing is as important to me as my dancing. Neither is anything as important to you as your music. Is it, Sebastian?'

He didn't answer, but stood looking out at the snowy hills.

'As I was saying when you barged in about your silly *tutu* – it's beautiful out there, isn't it? You'll come back here to Northumberland, you know, Veronica.'

'How can I?' I laughed. 'My work is in London.'

'Oh, I didn't mean next week, or even next year. I meant – just *some day*. How long can a dancer go on dancing?'

'Till they're about thirty,' I answered. 'Sometimes longer. It all depends upon how hard they're worked.'

'Well, when you're in the sear and yellow – about thirty – you'll come back,' laughed Sebastian. 'You'll come back here to Northumberland. You'll find you have to – your mother was Northumbrian. Once a Northumbrian, always a Northumbrian! Perhaps you'll marry a North Countryman and have children. Then they'll be North Country, born and bred – instead of only born, like you!'

'You are funny, Sebastian,' I said. 'What about you? *You're* Northumbrian, and yet you're dying to get to London, aren't you? You've always said so.'

'It's a case of needs must with me,' Sebastian assured me. 'I've got to go to London – and other places besides – for my training. But when I want to compose – when I really want to think things out – I'll come back here, you bet! One day, when I'm famous, and when I've made a lot of money, I shall be able to live here in my own home.' He cast a glance over his shoulder at the darkening hall with the pictures of his ancestors gleaming on its walls in the light of the dying fire; the oak staircase, its steps worn by the feet of his forebears. 'Some day I'll come back—'

It was then I realized for the first time that, although Sebastian joked about living in the gardener's cottage at the bottom of his own drive, and pretended he loved it, he didn't really. All the time he was feeling that Aunt June and Uncle John were interlopers and ought not to be living in the Hall. Of course, it wasn't their fault; in fact, they were doing Sebastian a good turn by keeping Bracken Hall in the Scott family, but that didn't alter the fact. They were living in his ancestral home.

'I believe you'll do as you say,' I said, looking at his tense face in the flickering firelight. 'I believe you'll do all you say.'

Chapter 17

The Telegram

THE next morning, soon after breakfast, the local dressmaker came up from the village to alter some of Caroline's and Fiona's school clothes, and I was left all on my own. I wandered down to the lake, realizing suddenly that I hadn't been there since I'd come back for the holidays – unless you could count the time we'd passed it on our way back from church on Christmas Eve. There was no one in sight except the distant figure of old Billy, the postman, trudging up the newly opened road from the village with the letters. I waved to him, and then went on my way down the little track through the fir plantation that Sebastian, Caroline, and I had dug. At the far side of the plantation, I left the track and set off towards the lake, picking my way round the drifts.

As I peeped into the boathouse and saw the same old bathing costumes draped stiffly round the sides of the little rowing-boat – I think most of them were frozen! – I had the same queer, dream-like feeling about London as I had had out on the moor the night we'd been lost in the snow. It seemed quite impossible that at this very moment, while I was standing in this silent place, thousands of people were scurrying on the Underground, jostling shoulders with thousands of other people.

I stared across the frozen lake to the island where Sebastian and I had gathered wild strawberries on my first morning at Bracken Hall – the morning I had run away and he'd made me come back. It seemed only yesterday, and yet what an awful lot of things had happened in between.

Suddenly there was the sound of low whistling.

'Hullo, Veronica!' said Sebastian's voice. 'Having a last look round?'

139

'Oh, not a last look,' I answered. 'I've still got more than a week's holiday left, you know. I was just seeing if Spotted Peril and Rhapsody in Stripes were still there. By the way how did you know I was here?'

'Saw you from the bathroom window,' said Sebastian. 'You were asking about the latest creations in swimwear? Well, Spotted Peril is still in the land of the living, but I'm afraid Rhapsody has gone the way of all flesh – in other words, it's dropped to pieces, so I cleaned my bike with it. Everything decays – even bathing costumes.'

'You are horrible!' I laughed. 'You always were. I'm sorry about Rhapsody in Stripes – it was like an old friend.'

'Even old friends have a habit of changing,' remarked Sebastian, playing Ducks and Drakes with a pebble on the frozen surface of the lake.

'What do you mean?'

'Well, you're different, you know, Veronica. You're here, and yet you're not here.'

'I don't know what you mean.'

'One foot in Bracken, the other in London,' Sebastian stated enigmatically. ' "Poised on tiptoe for a flight," as the poet johnny said. I forget which one, but it doesn't matter.' Then, with that queer insight that he so often showed, he added: 'I feel that every time you look at the lake, or the trees, or even the hills, you're thinking of some ballet or other.'

'I suppose *you* don't ever imagine things?' I retorted. 'Things to do with your music, I mean. I suppose *you* weren't thinking of this wood by the lake when you wrote your *Woodland Symphony*, Sebastian?'

He laughed.

'You've got me there, Veronica! I suppose I *was* thinking of all this' – he waved an arm, embracing the whole landscape of lake and woods beyond. 'Yes, you're right. I *was* thinking of it – among other things. But it doesn't alter what I said at first. You're different, Veronica.'

'As a matter of fact,' I said slowly, 'you're different, too,

Sebastian. You're much more grown up, and I don't think I like you as well.'

'We all have to grow up,' said Sebastian nonchalantly. 'I'm seventeen, you know – all but a fortnight. And as to whether you like me as well – it's all the same to me.'

'Oh, Sebastian, don't be offended,' I begged. 'I was only joking. You're always joking yourself, and you don't expect people to take you seriously, so why take *me* seriously?'

'Sometimes,' said Sebastian, 'there's a lot of truth in a joke. I felt there was quite a bit in that one. Come on – let's walk over to the island. The ice will bear us; I tried it the other night when I came back from church.'

We walked over to the island, and sat for a bit in the old duck-punt, moored among the reeds. It was all so white and frozen that it was almost impossible to believe that in just a few months' time the swans would again be busy making their nest among the rushes.

'A quarter past eleven!' said Sebastian, as the silvery chime of the stable clock reached us on the frosty air. 'You'll be late for your milk, Veronica! Trixie will be in a flap – feeding you up is a sort of religion with her! It's really funny, because no matter how much milk you drink, I don't believe you get one inch fatter!'

'I hope not!' I said with such a horror-stricken note in my voice that Sebastian burst out laughing.

Just as we reached the terraced walk in front of the house we were met by Caroline. She seemed to be in a state of great excitement.

'Oh, Veronica!' she panted. 'I've been looking for you simply everywhere. There's a telegram for you. It came through by phone, and Trixie tried to take it down, but she said she couldn't make head or tail of it – it was about the Bible!'

'The Bible!' I laughed. 'Oh, no – it couldn't have been.'

'Well, Trixie said it was, and she told the exchange she'd

fetch you, and then we couldn't find you, so the exchange said they'd ring up again in ten minutes. Do come quickly!'

'Right-ho!' I said. 'I expect it's nothing the least bit important. I can't understand about the Bible, though. I expect Trixie's got it wrong – she's a bit deaf, you know, though she won't admit it.'

'You get along, then,' said Sebastian. 'I'm going round to the stables to see Warrior. Oh, by the way, Veronica. I've written out that music the way you said you wanted it – the Czardas, you know. We can try it over some time. So long!'

He strode away stablewards, and Caroline and I dashed into the house. Just as we got to the hall, the phone rang again. I took up the receiver, and a bored voice at the other end said: 'Is that Bracken 394? A telegram for you. Are you ready? ... "To Weston, Bracken Hall, Northumberland. Return rehearsal *Job* Saturday 2 o'clock Covent Garden. Important. Willan." ... Shall I repeat that?'

'Yes, please!' I begged, my head spinning. 'What was that you said about *Job*? Are you *sure* you said *Job*?'

'J-O-B,' said the voice at the other end, sounding more bored every minute. 'J for Jack, O for Oliver, B for Benjamin.'

'Thank you,' I said feebly. 'No, you needn't send it on by post. Goodbye.'

I put down the receiver and stood lost in thought. What on earth could it mean? ... *Job*? ... I knew there was a ballet by that name, but what had it got to do with me? Surely, surely I couldn't have got a part in it? And yet it was certainly from the school – the signature, Willan, told me that. I simply couldn't believe it. I began to wonder if I'd heard the telephone operator rightly, and to wish that I'd had the telegram sent on to me, after all. But no – it would have been too late, anyway – the wire said a rehearsal at two o'clock on Saturday. That was tomorrow. I'd have to go back by sleeper tonight ... Thoughts raced round in my head ...

'What's the matter, Veronica?' Caroline's voice, sounding

anxious, woke me out of my daydream. 'Has anything happened?'

'Yes – no – I don't know,' I stammered. 'Really, I don't know what to think.'

'I wonder if this will help,' Caroline said, holding out a letter. 'Billie brought it a bit ago. It's for you, and it's from London.'

'It's from Sara,' I said, tearing open the letter. 'I don't suppose it has anything to do with the wire.'

But it had!

Dear Veronica, [wrote Sara]. Something frightfully thrilling has happened. We had a rehearsal of the Youth Festival thing on Christmas Eve at School, and right in the middle of it, who should walk in but Madame! Yes, Madame herself – silver-fox furs and all! She stopped the rehearsal, and began to talk to Miss Willan. Well, it seems that one of the Sons of the Morning in Madame's ballet, *Job*, has sprained her ankle, and all the understudies have been used up already because of the epidemic of flu, so Madame came along to get someone from the school. It's not a part just anyone can do. For one thing, they have to have a boyish figure and look young, and for another they have to be musical. You see, the time of Vaughan Williams' music is most awfully tricky. Madame knew a Wells student would manage it OK, though, because we've all been trained in Eurhythmics. Imagine her shock when she found out that practically everyone, except the people who had parts already in the Theatre Ballet, and Taiis, who's dark-skinned, was in the Finsbury Park thing that's on exactly when *Job* is! I don't think she was too pleased, though of course it was no one's fault.

Well, when she was safely away. I plucked up my courage and went up to Miss Willan – oh, I know it was awful cheek, because naturally I wasn't supposed to be listening, but things were desperate. Well, I went up to her and said:

'Oh, Miss Willan – Veronica isn't in the Youth Festival.' And she said: 'You mean Veronica Weston? And why isn't she in it?' Then I explained about your watch being slow, and you missing the audition, and she said, half to herself: 'Veronica is quite good at Eurhythmics, isn't she?' And I said: 'She's by far the best in the class, Miss Willan, and she's ever so small; I mean, she'd make a marvellous boy for a Son of the Morning.' Well, after this she rushed out, and I guessed she was going to catch Madame before she left the school. After a bit she came back and asked for your address, and said she was going to send you a wire. So, though it isn't definitely fixed yet, I think you'll get the part all right. It'll be wonderful for you, because, being Madame's own ballet, naturally she's especially interested in it; she even comes to some of the rehearsals. Oh, Veronica – I'm so *thrilled*, because I know how much you want to be in something!

Lots of love, Sara.

PS. I heard Willan talking to Serge and asking him whether he thought you'd be right for the Farandole in *The Sleeping Beauty*, because Jocelyn, the girl who's sprained her ankle, was in that too. He said he expected you would, so you'll most likely get that part too. Guess who your partner will be? Toni Rossini! Cheerio! Sara.

When I had finished the letter I read it all through again; then I gave a yell.

'Caroline! Trixie! Aunt June! Everybody! I've got it! I've got it at last! I'm actually in something! Oh, Caroline – I'm so happy!'

Then I remembered that Sebastian wasn't there, and, above all, I wanted Sebastian to hear my wonderful news.

'I must just dash down to the stables,' I shrieked, 'and tell Sebastian.' I seized Caroline round the waist, and waltzed her round. Then I dashed away, leaving her staring after me in

144

utter bewilderment, for of course she didn't know what I'd got, or what I was in. It might be a prize for a sweepstake, for all she knew!

'Sebastian!' I yelled, as soon as I came within shouting distance of the stables. 'Sebastian! Where are you?'

Sebastian had just finished mucking-out the stable. He had tied Warrior up to a ring in the wall outside the door, and now he emerged, dandy-brush in hand, to see what the row was about.

'Well, why the shrieks and yells?'

'Oh, Sebastian!' I said, half laughing, half crying. 'My phone call – guess what it was about!'

'Search me! Haven't an earthly.'

'It was to tell me to go back to London tonight. I've got a part in *Job*, and another in *The Sleeping Beauty*. At least, I'm almost sure I have, and the rehearsal's tomorrow at two, so I shall have to get a sleeper and go back tonight. And my partner in the Farandole – he's Toni Rossini. You remember – the boy I told you about – my dancing partner. It will be marvellous to dance with him again, and besides, he's a real choreographer. He's had several ballets produced, and I shall actually be dancing with him on Covent Garden stage! Oh, Sebastian, isn't it wonderful?'

'Wonderful,' said Sebastian flatly.

Something in his voice pulled me up with a jerk.

'What's the matter? Why do you say "wonderful" like that? – as if you weren't a bit pleased. *Aren't* you pleased?'

'Take it as said,' answered Sebastian, turning to his pony, and making a great play with the dandy-brush.

Then, with a funny feeling in my inside, I remembered.

'Oh, Sebastian, I'm so sorry – I – I'm afraid I forgot – I completely forgot all about your concert.'

'Oh, don't let that worry you,' said Sebastian frigidly.

'I'm frightfully sorry,' I said, some of my happiness evaporating. 'But even if I *had* remembered, I couldn't have done anything about it, could I?'

'No, of course not,' agreed Sebastian.

'You don't think – surely you couldn't think I ought not to go back tonight?' I said incredulously. Then, as he didn't answer, I burst out: 'You know quite well I've *got* to go back. It's my career. You'd go back if it were *your* career, wouldn't you, Sebastian?'

'Of course. I'm a man.'

'What difference does that make?'

'Quite a lot,' Sebastian said, turning his back on me, and grooming Warrior with great deliberation. 'Men are forced to have careers. Women don't have to; they just barge into them. It's just silly for a woman to give up everything – friends, beauty sleep, peace of mind – even marriage – for a stupid thing like ballet.'

'It's not stupid!' I yelled, almost crying. 'It's my *life*!'

'Then it ought not to be,' declared Sebastian.

I stared at him aghast.

'You never used to think like this before.'

'Well, I do now. Goodbye, Veronica.'

'What do you mean – saying "goodbye, Veronica" like that? What about tonight? You're playing for me tonight at Lady Blantosh's concert, don't forget.'

'Oh, no I'm not,' stated Sebastian. 'If you decide to go back to London tonight, then *I* decide here and now not to make a mug of myself and play your stupid dances for you.'

'But you *promised* to play them,' I wailed. 'It's all arranged that you should play them. I can't do them if you don't play for me.'

'That's just too bad,' drawled Sebastian. 'Why should I play it for you when you calmly walk out on my concert? You walk out on me – OK. I walk out on you. Where's the difference?'

'You know it's different altogether,' I argued desperately. 'If I don't turn up at that rehearsal tomorrow, I shall lose the part altogether. It might be the turning-point of my whole career. As for your concert – it doesn't matter a scrap whether

I'm there or not. It's *you* that matters for your concert, Sebastian. Oh, can't you see that?'

'How do you know it doesn't matter?' he answered. 'How do you know I'm not playing for you, Veronica? How do you know I haven't written my *Woodland Symphony* especially for you – inspired by your grace, your funny remote face, the lovely way you move—'

I just stared at him, puzzled.

'I don't know what you mean.'

'Are you still going back tonight?'

'You know I must,' I answered.

'Very well . . .'

He left Warrior and went back into the stable. When he returned, he carried a small roll of music in his hand.

'Then, we won't need this.' He unrolled the sheets and tore them across and across. The pieces fluttered to the ground and lay between us.

'Oh, Sebastian! What have you done?'

'You remember that day, out on the moors, I told you I was in love with somebody,' Sebastian said, turning away from me. 'Well, it wasn't a joke – it was true. I was in love with you – you, Veronica. When I said goodbye to you tomorrow night, I was going to kiss you. I thought you were the nicest girl I'd ever met.'

I was so surprised that for a moment I said nothing at all. Then I burst out: 'How dare you say that! I wouldn't have let you kiss me.'

'You wouldn't have had any choice,' declared Sebastian, with a toss of his black head. 'I wasn't going to ask you first. When I decide to do a thing, I do it – I don't ask first. But don't worry,' he added. 'I shan't do it now. I don't even want to shake hands with you – let alone kiss you.'

'You're only a kid,' I retorted. 'We're both kids.'

'I'm almost seventeen,' he answered. 'Only a year younger than your friend, Stella, who's going to be married. But you're right – you *are* a kid, Veronica – a stupid, selfish little kid.

Some day perhaps you'll know better. Goodbye, Veronica.'

He unhitched Warrior from the ring, vaulted upon his back, and was away across the stable yard, and out into the field before I had time to reply. I watched him gallop across the snowy meadow, and round the straw stacks at the far side – he never once looked back.

I turned again to the empty stable. On the ground lay the bits of white paper with Sebastian's painstakingly written music upon them. I knew he'd sat up late after the party last night to do it, and I felt awful. But there was no question in my own mind as to what I must do. When you're a ballet dancer you put all else behind you – even friends and sweet-hearts, if you have a sweetheart. Your art must come first. I felt that Sebastian ought to understand that; after all, he was an *artiste* himself. But then, Sebastian had never been reason-able; had never acted or thought in a logical way; he was a law unto himself.

I carefully picked up some of the pieces of paper and put them in my pocket, though why I did it I don't know, for of course they weren't the least use to me, all torn like that. After this I went into the loosebox next door, where Arabesque was stabled, put my head down on his warm neck and began to cry; and, whether my tears were tears of sorrow, anger or frustration, I don't know. Perhaps a bit of all three. After a while I dried my eyes and went back to the house.

Caroline looked at my red eyes in amazement.

'Why, what on earth's the matter, Veronica? I thought you were so happy—'

'So I was,' I said, with a sniff of self-pity, 'and so I am still – in one part of me. But I'm terribly miserable in the other part. You see, Sebastian is furious with me. I f-forgot all about his c-concert, and now he won't p-play for me.' I began to cry again.

Caroline didn't know what to say. Unfortunately, I hadn't noticed that Fiona was standing by the window.

'Well, now perhaps you know what Sebastian is really like,'

she said with a hateful sneering note in her voice. 'You've been a long time finding out, I must say. I always *told* you how unreliable and selfish he was.'

'He's not unreliable and selfish!' I yelled at her. 'He's – he's – oh, I don't know what he is. It's me who's selfish; I know I am, but I can't help it – I've got to go.'

I seized the telephone and rang up Newcastle Central Station. They put me through to the reservation bureau, and a girl answered my inquiry. No, they hadn't got a first-class sleeper for tonight, but they could give me a third-class.

'All right – I'll have that,' I said. After all, what did it matter if I travelled first class or third? What did it matter if I got a sleeper at all? I shouldn't sleep a wink, anyway.

Chapter 18

Journey Back to London

I WAS right! I didn't sleep much that night. My berth was a top one, and when the train slid away from the platform, and had gathered up speed, I climbed wearily up into my bunk. The other three people in the compartment were evidently friends, for they talked, and laughed, and exchanged sweets and biscuits. I gathered from their conversation that they'd come up from the south to a friend's wedding, and were now on their way home. The girl on the upper berth opposite stared at me curiously. I think I must have looked very woebegone, for she said kindly:

'Leaving home for the first time, eh? Keep your pecker up, kid! Have a chocolate cream?'

At any ordinary time I'd have accepted the offer gratefully – chocolate creams being favourites of mine. But tonight the very sound of them made me feel sick.

'No, thank you,' I said. Then, as she repeated her offer more pressingly, I added: 'Really, I couldn't. Thanks awfully, all the same.'

'OK,' she said cheerfully. 'Have it your own way. But take my word for it, you'll get used to it, kid. Leaving your ma for the first time is awful, but it'll pass off. Can't live at home, tied to Mammy's apron-strings all your life, you know. Got to go out into the wide world some day. What's your job, kid?'

'I – I'm a dancer,' I stammered.

'A dancer? What sort? Tap, and the splits I suppose?'

'No – I'm a ballet dancer,' I answered.

'Ah – ballet? Been in the panto, eh? Good show at the Empire this year. My sister lives down at Byker, and she took all the kids in the Christmas hols. Where are you going to dance now?'

'C-Covent G-Garden,' I gulped.

If I had wished to cause a sensation, I certainly did so. The two other girls came right out of their bunks, and all three stared at me as if I were a rare orchid in a botanical garden.

'You don't say!' said the girl opposite me. 'What's your name, dearie? Moira Shearer?'

I suppose there was some excuse for their not believing me. Anything less like the popular idea of a glamorous ballet dancer than me, with my red eyes and woebegone expression, you couldn't have found. But I didn't feel it was worth the bother of trying to convince them, so I lay down under my rug and tried to go to sleep.

I was very tired after the concert and all the excitements of the day but, try as I would, I couldn't sleep. Perhaps I was *too* tired; or perhaps I was too miserable. Anyhow, my thoughts kept going round and round in my head, and I kept living over again the events of the last few hours – the awful rush I'd had finding gramophone records that I could dance to as a substitute for Sebastian's playing; unpacking the peasant costume that I now wouldn't need; doing my packing for to-night, because I was going straight from the village hall to the station.

I saw again the crowded room, and heard Lady Blantosh's kind voice announcing that : 'Now little Veronica Weston will dance for us. Veronica, as I expect you all know, is a pupil at a very famous dancing school called Sadler's Wells. I'm sure you are all simply longing to see her dance. I know *I* am!'

I danced very badly. All the time, instead of losing myself in the lovely music, I was seeing Sebastian's face when he'd said : 'Oh, don't let it worry you!' Fortunately, the people at the concert weren't the sort of people to notice that I had lost my *ballon;* that my *pointes* wobbled; that my dancing was strained and unhappy. They clapped me just as loudly as if I had been Margot Fonteyn herself, and for that I was grateful.

151

As I huddled under the railway company's prickly rug, I lived again the long drive to the station along roads piled high with snow on either side. Sometimes Perkins had to get out of the brake and dig, and I got out and helped him. Then he'd tell me to 'get back into the car, and keep warm'. Once, when we'd cleared away an especially big drift, and Perkins had stood leaning on his shovel in the glare of the headlights, I felt a flood of gratitude towards him sweep over me.

'Oh, Perkins – it is perfectly *sweet* of you to do this for me,' I said. 'Really, it's just wonderful the way people keep on doing things for me.'

'Well, miss,' said Perkins, wiping his face with a red and white spotted hankie and getting back into the driving seat, 'I sees it this way. When you comes to Bracken, you offers to get out of the car and open the gates for me. That was the very first thing you does. Remember? "*I'll* do it, Perkins!" you says. "Don't you bother, Perkins," you says. Well, I says to myself that very day – if I can do anything for that youngster, you bet I will! And I'm not one to forget my promises. So that's how it is. There's some people,' added Perkins, 'as gets things done for 'em all their lives, and some 'as don't. You're one of the first class, Miss Veronica.'

Desperately I tried to think of the exciting thing that had happened to me – my part in *Job*, and the Farendole that I was going to dance with Toni, but all I could think of was Sebastian's voice saying: 'I thought you were the nicest girl I'd ever met ... I don't even want to shake hands with you now, let alone kiss you ... You're just a selfish kid; perhaps some day you'll know better ... Goodbye, Veronica ...'

'Goodbye,' the whirring of the wheels echoed sadly. 'Goodbye ... goodbye ... Veronica ...'

Chapter 19

Dress Rehearsal of *Job*

IT was fortunate, perhaps, that I had so much to do during the next few weeks that I had no time to think. Only at nights, when Mrs Crapper and I listened-in to the wireless, did my thoughts stray back to Northumberland. Sometimes the cry of a curlew, given as a 'signature' to a country programme, or the sounds of sheep bleating, or the clip-clop of a horse's hooves on the hard road, would bring back to me memories of Bracken Hall, and I would rush out of the room or turn off the radio. I expect Mrs Crapper wondered what was the matter with me, but she never asked any questions. In some ways she was the soul of diplomacy, was Mrs Crapper!

I went to the rehearsal of *Job* on the Saturday afternoon of my return, and got the part of the Son of the Morning who had dropped out. Madame was there herself, and I could feel her watching me to see if I would pass muster. It was a terrifying feeling, because Madame has eyes that not only look *at* you, but *through* you, as well, in a most disconcerting way. Still, I did feel, when I was told that I had got the part, that I must have shown up quite well. Automatically I got the part in the Farandole out of *The Sleeping Beauty*, too. Toni was very helpful, as usual, and, with his assistance, I managed not to disgrace myself.

The weeks sped away and, before I knew it, the day of the dress rehearsal of *Job* dawned. I'd had a letter from Stella and Jonathan in which they said that they weren't coming back to London before the wedding, which was to be in one week's time, and they wanted me to go north for it and be bridesmaid. I wrote back and explained that I couldn't because of *Job*, and really I was quite glad to have the excuse. I didn't feel like going back to Northumberland again just yet! So as it turned out, Mrs Crapper was the only person to wish me luck upon the eventful day. Miss Broadbent, the lady who was secretary to the corset manufacturer, wished me good morning on the stairs, but I'm pretty sure it wasn't anything to do with my rehearsal, but merely a 'conventional greeting', as they say.

I looked round me with shining eyes as I followed the others up the endless flight of stone stairs to our dressing-room. Although by now I had been in a real dressing-room several times, yet I was still thrilled by everything – even the notice on the door: CHORUS LADIES! For the sake of those people who have never been inside a theatrical dressing-room, I will tell you what ours was like. It was a long room, and all round the walls were narrow tables with mirrors behind them. Down the middle of the room were more tables and mirrors. There were two of us to each mirror, and I shared mine with Dorothea. We wrote our names on opposite corners of our mirror with greasepaint. Above the mirrors were shelves where you could put your clothes, make-up, and personal belongings. Some of the girls stuck photographs round the sides of their mirrors – pictures of their families, sometimes, but more often of their favourite ballet or film star. All the costumes were kept on stands and carefully looked after by dressers, and woe betide you if you threw one of them on the floor!

It took me a long time to get ready for *Job*. Not that the Son of the Morning costume was at all complicated. It consisted of a silk tunic, curled wig, and a pair of huge silver wings which were the bane of our lives. I dare say they looked wonderful from the audience, but to us, who had to wear them, they were awful. They were made of silvered wire, and after you'd worn them for about five minutes they felt as if they weighed at least a ton! Although they were padded, they still hurt your shoulders. As for dancing in them – well, now I understand why our part wasn't considered a 'dancing part'. It would have been quite impossible to dance in those wings!

Well, so far so good. As I say, the costume was quite easy to get on, even if it wasn't exactly comfortable. The trouble was that our legs were bare, so we had to cover ourselves with wet-white as far up as the thighs. Our arms and shoulders had to be done, too; so really, as someone said, there wasn't much of us that *wasn't* whitewashed! The wet-white was frightfully messy to put on, and it was even more messy to take off, as I found to my cost after the dress rehearsal. Also, my wig happened to be several sizes too small for me and, besides giving me a headache, I had a fight to the death every time I put it on! But as there wasn't a bigger one to spare, and I was an outsider, naturally I had to be the one to 'make do'.

Job, I must explain, is a rather unusual production – not a bit like the general idea of a ballet. There is no *pointe*-work in it; indeed, most of the characters dance with bare feet or wearing sandals. The ballet is all in two parts – earthly and spiritual. The earthly part, which depicts Job with his children, and his struggles in the world, is danced on the front portion of the stage; the spiritual part at the back, on a flight of shining steps. At first, when I was just learning the part, I couldn't see how you could possibly dance on a flight of steps, no matter how broad they were, but I soon found out that you didn't really dance at all; you just moved about rhythmically, and you've no idea how difficult it is to move gracefully on a staircase in time to Vaughan Williams' music, which, though it's very beautiful, isn't a bit usual.

Another thing I found very queer, when I first began to dance on the real stage, was the arrangement of drop-curtains in conjunction with the lighting. It seemed strange to me to be standing in position on the heavenly staircase, along with crowds of other people, with only a flimsy gauze curtain between us and the audience, and yet know that all those people in the darkened auditorium couldn't see us, though we could see them quite plainly. For ages I felt like yelling: 'Look out! The audience can see you!' when the almost invisible curtain had slid silently between us and the house, and Satan did an *entrechat* behind it. I found it queer in *The Sleeping Beauty*, too, when Margot Fonteyn stood laughing behind the spider-web drop-curtain in the Vision Scene, seemingly in full view of the audience.

As I said before, Toni Rossini had been a great help to me during all these weeks of rehearsal. I expect it was a case of 'a fellow feeling makes us wondrous kind', because Toni was really in the Theatre Ballet, and he'd only been lent to the First Company for the season, so he was an outsider like me. He'd got quite an important part in *Job*, as well as the small part in the Farandole in *The Sleeping Beauty*.

'Will you go back to the Theatre Ballet as soon as this is over?' I asked him as we waited in the wings on that day of the dress rehearsal.

He nodded.

'Oh, yes; I write a new ballet for the Company.'

'Gosh! How exciting! What is it called?' I demanded.

'I call it *The Depths of the Sea*,' he answered. 'It is about a mermaid. I think of a particular person when I write it.'

'I know! Belinda?' I exclaimed.

He nodded again.

'Some day,' he said unexpectedly, 'I write a ballet for you, Veronique. You will be a very beautiful dancer. I can see it. You have an exquisite "line".'

I was so surprised that I blushed hotly. Finally, I stammered:

'Thanks, awfully, Toni; it's good of you to say so, and I hope you're right and that I do dance beautifully, but so far I don't feel I've got on much. I don't think anybody but you – and perhaps Gilbert – thinks much of my dancing.'

Toni was silent for a bit; then he said, in his stilted, too-perfect English:

'You mistake, Veronique. They think you good.'

'I imagined they did once,' I said with a sigh. 'But now – I don't know. Do you realize I'm still down in the Junior class with all the new girls.'

'You must have patience,' said Toni gravely. 'Sometimes

156

they keep a promising dancer back to acquire yet stronger technique before she attempt the more advanced work. I have seen it happen more than once. Perhaps it is so with you.'

I sighed again.

'Well, if they do that, why don't they *tell* you?' I burst out at length. 'Then you'd work like fury, instead of getting depressed and browned-off.'

Toni shrugged his shoulders expressively.

'I do not know. Perhaps they think that to tell you would make you swollen of the head, as you say in English. So they say nothing. You must think for yourself. If you are good – you know it. If you are not,' he shrugged again, 'you know it also.'

'That's all very well,' I said, 'but sometimes it's hard to go on believing in oneself.'

'Look – I tell you something,' Toni said, as if making a sudden resolution. 'Quite by accident this afternoon I hear *Madame la Directrice* and the *Maître-de-ballet* talk together. They stand on one side of a piece of stage scenery, I upon the other; I hear them talk before I know who it is who speak. Madame she say: "*That* one with the pale face and the big dark eyes" – that was you, Veronique – "that one," she say, "is the one to watch. I have a feeling that she will be a very great dancer, but of course – who knows?" Then she shrugged in her French way, though she is not French, but Irish!'

'Did she really say that?' I gasped, with a thrill of joy. 'Did she really? I just can't believe it! I expect it was someone else she meant, and not me at all; but thanks for telling me, all the same, Toni.'

'It was a pleasure,' said Toni, with a little bow.

As we stood there, in the wings, side by side, I stared at him curiously. It wasn't rude, because his eyes were on the dancers on the stage, and I'm quite sure he'd forgotten all about me. Toni had what you might call a gentle face, with the round forehead and large eyes of the poet and the dreamer. His mouth had a tender curve, uplifted at the corners, as if all the

157

time his thoughts were beautiful ones. There was none of the fire and driving force of Stcherbakof or Sebastian in Toni Rossini. None of the ruthlessness, and – yes, I must admit it, though I'd denied it indignantly to Fiona – the selfishness that predominated in the characters of those other two *artistes*. In a way, Toni was more like Jonathan, although nobody could have been less like Jonathan in outward appearance. Jonathan could have put Toni in his waistcoat pocket!

I felt, as I looked at Toni, that although he was a competent and graceful dancer and had been well trained, it was not as a dancer that he would make his name. He would be remembered, not by his own dancing, but by the lovely combinations of steps and figures he composed for other people; by his sense of beauty that showed in the 'line' of his creations; in the way he grouped his dancers against the backcloth; by the way his ballets lived with the music, so that you couldn't separate the one from the other. In other words, it was as a choreographer, and not as a dancer, that Toni Rossini would be remembered.

And I was standing in the shadowy wings of Covent Garden Theatre, side by side with this as yet unknown young man – a young man who would fling the torch of his creative genius on to the dry bones of ballet and set them ablaze, just as Massine had done, and Robert Helpmann. It was a thrilling feeling!

Suddenly my dreams were shattered. There were shouts on the stage; figures came crowding into the wings.

'It is time for you to go,' said Toni's soft voice in my ear. 'See, the curtain has fallen; you must be ready for your scene.'

Chapter 20

The End of the Season

I GOT a repertoire for the ballet season at Covent Garden and saw that *Job* was to run for two months, together with *The Sleeping Beauty*. Usually *Job* was on twice each week, while *The Sleeping Beauty* was performed five times – counting Saturday matinée. Occasionally there was a week when other ballets predominated, and I would only dance once in *Job* and a couple of times in *The Sleeping Beauty*, but as a general rule it was the *Job* and *Sleeping Beauty* season. I got five shillings a performance for *Job*, and ten shillings for *The Sleeping Beauty*, because the Farandole, although a much easier part than one of the Sons of the Morning, was a 'dancing part'. All my first week's pay went on make-up, and after that I spent most of my earnings on meals, because I found that it was quite impossible to get back to Heather Hill between performances and rehearsals – not to mention school! There were times, I can tell you, when I wished that Mrs Crapper's apartment house was a little nearer Covent Garden!

The weeks simply flew by, and, before I knew it, we were at the end of the season. I wrote to Caroline, apologizing for not having written before.

Dear Caroline [I said in my letter]. I expect you'll be thinking awful things about me for not having told you about my exciting experience on Covent Garden stage. To my shame I realize that I've only written to you once since I came back to London after the holidays. My only excuse is the usual one – work! Really, I haven't had a minute to call my own since I got back that Saturday morning. You see, the school makes no allowance for you when you get small parts in the ballets. I mean, you aren't excused any classes on that account – only if they happen to be at the exact time of the rehearsals. So I've been at school from nine-thirty every morning, which means leaving here soon after eight o'clock, and I haven't got back most nights till after eleven! The few nights when I haven't been on, I've just crawled home, too tired to do anything but swallow my supper, and fall into bed. All the same, it's been grand, and I wouldn't have missed it for anything. The Youth Festival people have been green with envy at me going off to Covent Garden every night.

Well, last night was the last performance of the season. And what fun it was! It ended with Margot Fonteyn as Princess Aurora in *The Sleeping Beauty*; Violetta Elvin – she used to be Prokhorova, you know, before she got married – as the Lilac Fairy, and Michael Soames as the Prince. They all danced wonderfully, and of course Margot excelled herself – she always does at a time like that! At the end of the performance she got so many flowers you couldn't see her for them. Someone passed a bottle of milk up for the White Cat, and indeed everyone was so happy, and in such good tempers, that you felt you were dancing on air, and not on a stage at all! Madame was in the staff box, and she was smiling like anything, and being so gracious to everybody. At the end of Farandole – that's the thing I dance with Toni Rossini – Toni put his arm round my waist, lifted me off my feet, and carried me right across the stage and out into the wings. Yes, in full view of the audience! But, of course, *they'd* think it was all part of the dance, and even if they hadn't, nobody would have cared! That was the sort of night it was!

And now it's all over. The Company are having ten days' holiday before they go on tour on the Continent. As for me, it's real hard work from now on. I simply must show Miss Willan and Gilbert that I'm made of the stuff they thought I was made of when they accepted me for the school. I don't

expect to get any more parts until the late summer when the
First Company is back again, except perhaps an odd one
down at Sadler's Wells.

Oh, Caroline – I *do* hope I've been all right in the small
parts I've had!

Lots of love, Veronica.

PS. I bought a seat for dear Mrs Crapper in the grand tier
out of my weekly earnings, and she saw *Job*. I think she'd
have liked *The Sleeping Beauty* better, as it's more usual,
but I simply couldn't get a ticket for it – it's so popular, and
I hadn't time to queue for one. Anyway, she said: 'It
seemed funny to me, Miss Veronica, all them people out of
the Bible, as real as real, and that poor old man' – she meant
Job – 'a settin' there, as patient as patient, and nothin' but
bad things rainin' down upon him like the doodlebugs on
London! I liked that bit fine when Satan rolled headlong
down the steps. Thrilling, that was! Poor young man! I
wonder what he does for his bruises? Someone ought to tell
him about that wonderful embrocation me Aunt Emily used
on me Uncle Henry before he died. I liked your wings fine,
Miss Veronica – not that I could see which one you was, me
eyes not being as good as they were, and all of you so alike,
but they looked nice, like that picture on the front of me
prayer-book.'

PPS. If I ever get as far as dancing a principal role at
Covent Garden in the dim, dim future – and I can tell you
it doesn't seem very likely at present – but if I ever do, I'll
book seats for you all. At least, all of you except Sebastian,
and I don't suppose he'd want to come. What fun it would
be, wouldn't it?

V

PPPS. I remember you once said that my letters were all
postscripts, so I may as well live up to my reputation, and

add yet another one. It's about Jonathan and Stella. They were married last month, and it was supposed to be a very quiet wedding, with *no* fuss, and absolutely no one knowing about it. But of course the papers ferreted it out – they *would*! Jonathan's estates grew in size with each account, and poor Stella became more and more lowly, until finally it appeared in the *Daily Courier* like this:

King Copetua and the Beggar-maid

Whirlwind romance between knight and obscure ballet dancer culminated last Friday in the marriage, at a tiny village church at the foot of the Cheviot Hills, of Jonathan Rosenbaum, the world-famous artist and sculptor, and Stella Mason, beautiful eighteen-year-old dancer, recently of the Sadler's Wells Ballet Company. The uninitiated may not be aware that the name Rosenbaum cloaks the identity of no less a personage than Sir Jonathan Craymore, the knightly owner of vast estates at Ravenskirk on the Scottish Border.

When I showed the account to Mrs Crapper, she was most impressed.

'Well I never!' she exclaimed. 'To think of our Mr Jonathan owning all that land! It just goes to show!'

What it went to show I really don't know, nor I'm sure did Mrs Crapper!

The bride [went on the awful journalist], is the granddaughter of Mary Mason and the late Joshua Mason of the tiny hamlet of Broomyhough at the foot of the Cheviots in Northumberland. Mrs Mason – 'Granny', as she is known locally – seated at her rustic table in her primitive kitchen, with the barnyard fowls wandering in and out around her feet, and an uncouth shepherd lad lounging on the deal settle by the fire, told me that her

162

granddaughter had met her young husband only a few days before the ceremony. She confessed that her granddaughter felt a certain amount of awe at the prospect of becoming Lady Craymore.

I must tell you, Caroline, that when I'd finished the article, I couldn't help feeling glad that Jonathan was safely away in Cornwall on his honeymoon. I'm quite sure he'd have been simply *furious*. Jonathan hates anything like that. However, I suppose journalists have to earn their livings like everybody else. This really *is* the end of my letter and its postscripts!

Love again, Veronica.

Chapter 21

A Class with Madame

AFTER the ballet season at Covent Garden had ended, nothing much happened to break the monotony of school life. There were small excitements, of course. For instance, Belinda's name began to appear in the picture papers and dancing magazines ...

This promising seventeen-year-old dancer, Belinda Beaucaire, as the Mermaid in the new ballet, *The Depths of the Sea*, especially created for her by Toni Rossini, the rising young choreographer. This ballet, by the way, was inspired by the famous picture by Burne-Jones, and is a perfect vehicle for this ballerina's Titian-haired, green-eyed beauty ... The classic beauty of the red-haired Belinda Beaucaire ... ballet dancer's meteoric rise to fame ... Belinda Beaucaire's sparkle and charm ... if Belinda Beaucaire can acquire the necessary discipline ... Belinda Beaucaire danced the role with charm, but a slight hardness marred an otherwise interesting performance ...

Pictures of Belinda began to appear in the *Dancing News*, the *Ballet Weekly*, and other periodicals. Belinda in *arabesque*; in *attitude*. Belinda as the Sugar Plum Fairy, the little jewelled crown setting off to perfection her classic features. Belinda, one hand caught in the misty folds of her *Sylphides* dress; Belinda as one of the Little Swans in *Swan Lake*. One weekly picture paper even had Belinda on the cover, all in technicolour, in a jade *tutu*, flaming red hair, and green eyes!

We sighed enviously as the papers went the round of the dressing-room.

'Gosh! Mustn't it be wonderful to be Belinda! ... Think of having a ballet made up especially for you! ... Mustn't Belinda be happy!'

Yes, as we pored over the magazines littering the dressing-room table, and gazed at the pictures, we all imagined ourselves as Belinda, the newly risen star, the darling of thousands of adoring balletomanes.

Another person who provided a small sensation was Marcia Rutherford. One foggy morning, towards the middle of the term, when we were changing for our first class, the door opened and Marcia sauntered in. Since it was five minutes to the hour, and she was still in her outdoor clothes, everyone stared at her in astonishment.

'You 'ad bettaire be queek, Marcia Rutterford!' counselled Denise Lebrun, who was a French girl and new this term. Incidentally, she had more assurance than all the rest of us put together! 'Zees ees ze class of Gilbert, and you know what 'e ees like eef one ees late. *En tout cas* on-ly 'alf of ze class ees 'ere because of ze fog, so Gilbert weel be *en colère*, yes!'

Marcia didn't make the slightest movement to take off her grass-green coat with its many gilt buttons, or her flamboyant hat.

'Gilbert!' she said, with a snap of her fingers. 'What do I care about Gilbert Delahaye, or what he thinks?'

'He can be frightfully nasty if he likes,' I said. 'I advise you to buck up, Marcia.'

'Oh, really! You do, do you?' drawled Marcia. 'Well, let me tell you, all of you, that I'm through with being bullied, and ordered about, and treated like dirt by your Gilbert Delahayes, and your Willans, and your other rubbish. I've got a job.'

'What sort of a job?' we gasped. 'A dancing job?'

'Sure!' drawled Marcia, moving a bit of chewing gum from one cheek to the other. 'A real dancing job. I've been taken on

165

in the new American show *Dance for Poppa*. I start tomorrow at ten quid a week. Not bad, eh?'

'Oh, but that's not *real* dancing,' I commented. 'It's just musical-comedy stuff, with high heels and no clothes!'

'Real enough for me!' declared Marcia. 'Much I care, anyway! It's the dough I'm after. That's what I came to this mouldy hole for, if you want to know.' She cast a disparaging glance round the dressing-room. 'I put up with it just so's I could get a good job elsewhere.'

'Well, I think it's awful,' said Lily. 'It's just selling your art.'

'Much I care!' said Marcia again. 'Well, I'll leave you poor mugs to the mercy of your wrathful Gilbert. It's two minutes past the hour. Oh, boy! Two minutes. Won't he be mad! So long, folks!'

She took the chewing gum out of her cheek, and stuck it on the pictured face of Margot Fonteyn that someone had pinned up on the wall beside the door, and with that last act of revolt she was gone.

For a moment we were silent with shocked amazement. Then Denise burst into excited speech.

'I care not now eef Gilbert ees *en colère*! I care not eef he go oop in ze smoke!' she exclaimed. 'We 'ave rid ourselves of Marcia Rutterford. I care not now *what* 'appens!'

But even the irrepressible Denise didn't know just what *was* going to happen!

As Denise had forecast, Gilbert was in a filthy temper. He cast a jaundiced eye over the depleted lines of his class, and then began to lecture those of his students who had managed to turn up.

A little fog, declared Gilbert, should stop no serious-minded students from being punctual. On the contrary, went on Gilbert, it ought to make them all the more determined to be on time. Modern girls – and men too, pronounced Gilbert – have no idea about battling with the elements. A drop of rain, a spot of mist, a puff of wind, and everyone begins talking a lot of nonsense about floods, hurricanes, and goodness knows what! Imagine anyone, went on Gilbert, casting a glance at the murky darkness outside, imagine anyone not daring to venture out because of a slight mist: ... 'Turn on those lights!' snapped Gilbert. 'We will begin!'

We began, and had got as far as '*pliés* on the other side', when the door opened.

'Come in,' said Gilbert in a resigned voice. 'Pray don't apologize. I *like* a little interruption. Don't mind me; come right in ... *Battements tendus*, please. *Begin!*'

Three minutes later the door opened again.

'Ah!' said Gilbert. 'Some more brave spirits? Congratulations, Monica and Kathleen! So good of you to come! I do hope you were not inconvenienced by the fog ... As I said before, *battements tendus*, please. *Ready!*'

The class went on in this vein, Gilbert growing more furious underneath, and more sarcastic on top every second. We all wondered when the lava would crack, and the volcano erupt. It happened about twenty minutes after the class had begun. A small meek girl named Kalchine, whom Gilbert disliked for no reason at all except perhaps, that she *was* meek, pushed open the door softly; then, in her fright at Gilbert's dark frown, she shut it behind her with a nervous bang.

'Please, Mr Delahaye—' she began.

Gilbert cut her short with a lordly gesture.

'If one more person comes in late,' he threatened, 'just *one* more person, and says "please, Mr Delahaye, the fog..."' – here Gilbert raised his voice to a squeak and imitated what he intended to be the female intonation – 'I shall ...'

As he said the words, the door behind him opened yet again.

'*Get out!*' roared Gilbert in a frenzy, banging his stick on the floor so hard that the ferrule broke off and shot across the room. 'Get out! Stay out! Go *away*! This fog is just an excuse for you all to be late! If your heart was in your work, you would be on time. I will not have it! Get out of my class!

Then something in our horror-stricken faces made him swing round to see who or what had made us all freeze in our places like that game you play at school called 'Statues'. At the door, resplendent in silver-fox furs and a charming smile, stood Madame herself – Madame, the director of the Company. Behind her, like twin attendants on royalty stood Miss Willan and Miss Smails.

Fortunately, Madame had a sense of humour. Also I think she was very fond of Gilbert, and understood his queer ways.

'I stand corrected, Mr Delahaye,' she said sweetly. 'I make no excuses; I am very sorry I am late for class.'

Gilbert rose to the occasion.

'*Madame!*' he said, with what might be called reverence. Then he came forward with outstretched hand, motioning one of the girls to bring forward a chair, and another to relieve Madame of her fur cape and gloves. It happened to be me, and I placed them carefully over the back of a second chair.

Madame hadn't taken a class since I'd been at the Wells, so I was all excitement. I remembered the day when I'd sat in the empty dressing-room and dreamed about it, and now, it seemed, my dream was to come true at last. It was a frightening yet thrilling thought!

Often enough Gilbert had given us lectures on what to do, and what not to do, if ever Madame took class.

'You must not be nervous,' said Gilbert. 'Everyone is afraid of Madame, and that is all wrong. It is true that her eyes look through you in a strange, piercing way, but that is only because she is searching for talent – always searching for talent. If you are all tense and strained, she will be furious. You must relax!'

It was all very well for Gilbert to talk about relaxing, but now, as we arranged ourselves once more along the *barres*, I thought that he ought to take his own advice to heart! He was sitting on the platform, obviously in an agony of nerves. Every time any one of us did anything he knew Madame wouldn't like, the expression on his always expressive face was almost funny in its intensity.

Madame was a wonderful teacher – clear and decisive. When she told you to do anything out of the ordinary, she always explained the reason for it, and her reasons were always sound and well thought out. Of course, she had her fads – what great teacher has not? – but they were what you might call sensible fads. In short, after I had got over my awe of her. I can truthfully say that I enjoyed every minute of her class.

There were no more interruptions; no more latecomers, though the class was still nothing like complete. I have a shrewd idea that Miss Willan had posted a scout to intercept any more latecomers. It was unthinkable that anyone should break in upon Madame's class. As well break in upon an audience with the King!

To my surprise, I got quite a lot of attention. Several times Madame stopped beside me, and placed my arm or leg, or told me not to strain my shoulders. In the centre-work I was in the front row. Of course, this wasn't really such a very great honour, because most of the rest were new girls and weren't as advanced as I was.

At the end of the class, after we'd been dismissed and had made our curtsies, Madame went up to Gilbert and said in a voice we could all hear: 'Who is that child with the pale face and the big dark eyes? Yes, the one in the front row? I noticed her before; she was one of the Sons of the Morning in *Job*, wasn't she?'

A queer sound went rustling round the class. You couldn't really call it a gasp, because no one would have dared to gasp in Madame's class, but it was a definite sound for all that – a sound of positive awe.

'Veronica Weston,' said Gilbert in a clear voice, and I knew by the way he said it that he was glad Madame had noticed me.

'She's quite promising, Mr Delahaye,' said Madame graciously. 'Really, a very interesting class altogether. I congratulate you!'

169

I walked home that night in a seventh heaven of delight. Now, I knew quite definitely that what Toni had told me that day in the wings was really true, and that I *was* good.

When I got home there was a parcel for me from Caroline, and inside was a letter.

> Dear Veronica, [it said]. Thank you for your letter. Mummy and I didn't know what to get you for your birthday. Finally we thought that perhaps you'd like a scarf and gloves to match the Fair Isle twinset Mummy gave you at Christmas. So here it is! Oh, I know your birthday isn't till Monday, but I thought I'd send your present in good time, because it's horrible not to get remembered on your birthday. Trixie is sending her gift tomorrow, so you're *bound* to get something on the right day. Daddy says he's sending you a cheque and you can buy what you like with it.
>
> Everything is much the same here. I don't believe I ever told you about Sebastian's concert – the one you missed. It went off very well, and there was someone there – a Doctor Humphrey Messenger – who's a frightfully important person in the musical world. He seems to think that Sebastian is really good, and he's arranged for him to have an audition, or whatever you call it, for a scholarship to the Royal College of Music, on Monday the 30th April. That's your birthday; isn't it funny!
>
> Will you be coming north during the summer hols, or will you be in a show?
>
> > Lots of love,
> >
> > CAROLINE

I sighed as I put down the letter. Somehow I knew that I wouldn't be seeing Northumberland that summer, or indeed for many summers to come.

Chapter 22

My Sixteenth Birthday

SARA, by the way, had just got a temporary job on television, so she'd left Sadler's Wells School. She got well paid for her work, so she was very cheerful. In fact, there was only one fly in Sara's ointment, and that was her mother. Sara's mother was what is called 'possessive'. She couldn't and wouldn't believe that Sara was really sixteen and could look after herself. When Sara had been at school, Mrs Linklater had known the times of all the classes, and woe betide poor Sara if she was five minutes late home from one of them! She daren't even drop into the ABC or Forte's for a cup of tea. When Sara had a dress rehearsal, or a performance at the theatre, Mrs Linklater sat in the dressing-room with her knitting, which was never anything exciting like Fair Isle, but something strictly utilitarian, like vests or dishcloths. As somebody said – it was just like the comic song: 'And mother came, too!' It was really amazing that Mrs Linklater stopped short at the dressing-room, or the wings, and didn't venture right out on to the stage, knitting and all! Someone else said sarcastically that Sara's name on the programme ought, by rights, to read: 'Sara Linklater – and mother.'

Well, we all have our crosses to bear, and even I, in my moment of triumph, still had that nagging ache, dulled now, it's true, but still there for all that – that ache that the name of Sebastian, or Northumberland, or even the mention of a symphony concert, brought to my heart. I felt that never, never would Sebastian forgive me for what I had done. He would always bear me a grudge because of that concert of his.

As I left the Underground on the Monday morning, the

morning of my sixteenth birthday, and walked past St Paul's
School along Colet Gardens, I thought of Sebastian – Sebastian playing for me for *my* first concert; Sebastian sucking the
wound when I'd been bitten by an adder, or thought I had;
Sebastian riding with me through the fog to catch the London
train, the night before my audition. And now Sebastian was
coming up to London for *his* audition this very day. How I
wished I could have said 'good luck' to him, as he's said it to
me that night so long ago on the platform of Newcastle
Central Station! But it was no use wishing . . .

My thoughts were still far away in Northumberland when I
walked across the Winter Garden and opened the dressing-
room door. There was a sudden hush when I walked in, as if
they'd all been talking about me.

'What's the matter?' I said absently. 'Has anything happened?'

'You've been sacked – turfed out,' said Monica, leaving the
glass, and perching herself on the edge of the table.

The room swam before my eyes. Then I heard the voice of
Denise exclaiming in rapid French; felt her arm round me.

'*Mon Dieu! Mon Dieu! Que faire? Ells se trouve mal!* She
ees going to faint! Monique, *tu es véritablement imbécile! La
pauvre petite – elle prend au serieux!*'

'Veronica – it's all right,' came the voice of Monica, serious
now and frightened. 'You aren't sacked really – it was only a
joke. *Please* don't faint. You're turned out of the Junior class.
That's all I meant. You're in the Senior. Madame's orders!
Please, please don't faint!'

'It's all right,' I said weakly. 'I don't know what made me
do that. I'm OK now.'

'You know you are a foolish one,' said Denise, smoothing
back my hair. 'Eef you are turned out – sacked as they say –
we in ze dressing-room would not be the first to know eet. Of a
surety not!'

'No, of course not,' I said with a wry smile. 'Only here, in
this school, you never know. You're always wondering, fearing,

172

and in a way *expecting* to be turned out, and when you said – by the way, Monica, what exactly *did* you say?'

'I said you'd been sacked!' laughed Monica. 'And so you have – sacked from the Junior class. And you're in the *pas-de-deux* class, *and* the Advanced Mime, *and* the Theatre class.'

'Oh, no! I can't believe it,' I said with shining eyes.

'It's gospel,' put in June. 'I heard Miss Willan telling Gilbert about it, and Gilbert said: "I'm darned glad! That kid has worked well. She's got guts. She deserves to get on, and besides – there's *something about her*!" And when he said that, Willan nodded and said: "I agree there's something about her. I shouldn't be surprised if—" Then they saw me; I wasn't really listening either. I just happened to be going down the corridor while they were talking. But anyway, they shut up after that.'

'Well, I'll miss having you in the front row to follow,' said Delia. 'It saved me a lot of trouble, and besides, I *liked* watching you, Veronica. I don't know how it is, but you're such a nice person to watch.'

'Thank you,' I said gratefully. Really I had quite a lot of friends in the Junior class. I felt almost sorry to be leaving it; though, of course, it would be glorious to be with the Seniors.

'I must find out what time my new classes are,' I said, getting up from the bench where Denise had pushed me. 'Of course, they'll all be different.'

'Are you sure you're OK?' Monica asked anxiously. 'You still look pale.'

'I'm always pale,' I laughed. 'Didn't you hear Madame call me "that pale child"! But I feel quite all right now; in fact, I feel grand.' I executed an *entrechat-six* just to convince them.

'Well, you've a class at three today – Serge,' June said – June always knew everything. 'And then there's RAD with Gilbert after that, and then you've a class with Willan five-fifteen to six, I think. So you've just a quarter of an hour for tea.'

'Then there's my performance down at Sadler's Wells at

173

In the pas de deux *class*

seven-thirty, and that means the theatre at six-thirty. Oh, dear! I had hoped to get home for tea,' I sighed. 'You see, it's my birthday.'

A chorus of voices wished me many happy returns of the day.

'Are you really sixteen, Veronica?' said June. 'Gosh! I can't believe it. You look such a kid. Well, I'm afraid your birthday tea will have to go west – like lots of other things when you decide to throw in your lot with the ballet.'

'Yes, but it's not as easy as all that,' I explained. 'I've asked Sara Linklater to tea, and she's on television now.'

'Well, ring her up,' suggested Monica.

'Yes, but *where*?'

'At the television place, of course. Why not?'

'I suppose I could do that,' I said rather doubtfully. 'I hope they won't mind.'

'What if they do?' said June with a shrug. 'They can't eat you!'

'No – but what about Sara?'

'Oh, well – they'll think all the more of her for having friends to ring her up,' declared June irrepressibly. 'That's my experience, anyway. People always think more of you if you cause them a lot of bother. It's human nature!'

'Um,' I said, still doubtfully. 'I suppose I shall have to do it, anyway.'

After morning school I dashed out to a kiosk and rang up the television studios, and got into touch with Sara. Like most things that you dread, it proved to be frightfully easy.

'Hullo!' came Sara's cheerful voice at the other end of the wire. 'Many happy returns of the day, Veronica!'

'Thanks awfully!' I answered. 'Look here, Sara, it's about my birthday I rang you up. I'm most awfully sorry, but I can't get back to tea today, after all. You see' – then I couldn't resist it – 'I've been turned out!'

There was a horrified silence at the other end. Then Sara burst out:

'Veronica – you *haven't*?'

'Yes I have!' I laughed. 'I've been turned out of the Junior class. Now I'm in the Senior, and the *pas-de-deux* class and everything else. Oh, Sara, I'm so happy! You just don't know how I feel.'

'Oh, yes I do,' said Sara at the other end, 'because I'm feeling that way myself. I've just been taken on to the permanent staff here. I'll tell you about it when we *do* meet. Let's have a special celebration, shall we? A double celebration!'

'Yes, let's,' I said. 'Oh, but what about your mother, Sara?—'

'Oh, I forgot to tell you with all the excitement,' came Sara's voice at the other end of the wire. 'Aunt Elizabeth's been taken ill and Mummy's had to go to her. Poor Mummy! She didn't know what to do. There was Aunt Elizabeth up in Birmingham, and me here in London, but in the end Auntie won. You see, when people are ill, Mummy just adores looking after them; she simply couldn't resist it!'

'Then let's go to the pictures next Saturday,' I said. 'I've nothing on – have you?'

'Not a thing.'

'Then let's go gay at the Marble Arch Pavilion. Uncle John sent me a cheque for my birthday. We'll have supper at Lyons afterwards.'

'I've got lots of money,' said Sara. 'This is a joint celebration. I pay half.'

'All right – if you like,' I agreed. 'Saturday, then, seven o'clock outside the Marble Arch Pavilion. Goodbye, Sara!'

'Goodbye!' said Sara at the other end. 'And you don't know how thrilled I am by your news, Veronica. I always knew you were frightfully good.'

I hung up the receiver, and dashed back to school. That night at eleven o'clock I let myself into 242 Heather Hill with my latch-key, and as I crawled wearily up the many stairs to my room I remembered suddenly that it was my birthday!

Epilogue: Enchanted Princess

THE terms passed. I began to get more and more small parts in the ballets. I went on tour with the Opera Ballet, and then on tour with the Theatre Ballet, or Second Company. Finally, the day I'd lived for all my life arrived, and I was really a member of the Company.

Time went on. I didn't rise to fame overnight, for no ballerina does, especially in the Sadler's Wells Company, where such a high standard of artistry is demanded. For a long time I worked away apparently unnoticed in the *corps-de-ballet*. I say 'apparently', because I learned afterwards that Madame (not my dear Madame Viret, but the Director of the Company) had been watching me closely all the time. At last I got a solo part. My photograph began to appear in the picture papers ... 'This promising young dancer, Veronica Weston ... Veronica Weston's classical line in the *pas-de-trois* from *Les Sylphides* ... a new ballet, *The Ice Maiden*, written especially for Veronica Weston by Toni Rossini whose choreography is attracting favourable notice from the critics ... Veronica Weston's charm and lyricism ...'

It was like Belinda all over again!

And Belinda? What of Belinda? She had shot ahead of me at first. She was the Serving-maid in *The Gods Go A-Begging*, while I was merely one of the Black Lackeys. She was Columbine in *Le Carnival*; I was Papillon. Finally, she was taken into the First Company at Covent Garden, and I took over her roles in the Second.

Then came the never-to-be-forgotten day when Madame singled me out and talked to me, and shortly afterwards I was taken into the First Company myself. Naturally, I watched

Belinda closely; she was my rival. She had been given roles, and she had danced them with charm and brilliance. But, as Madame Viret had prophesied long ago, something was stopping her further progress, and that something was her mind.

You see, as Madame Viret had said, you put something of yourself into every role you dance, and Belinda put her own coarse mind into her interpretations. Her 'line' and her classic beauty had drawn the attention of the undiscerning in the first place, but the critics knew that Belinda would never really 'arrive'. Photographs of her appeared less and less frequently in the papers; Press notices were confined to 'This role was danced brilliantly but rather hardly by Belinda Beaucaire ... A rather vulgar interpretation was given by Belinda Beaucaire.'

Yes, that was the trouble. When Belinda danced Columbine, the lady was not only a flirt, but a vulgar flirt. She over-mimed Swanilda in the ballet *Coppelia*, and made her seem vulgar too. Her dancing in *The Miracle of the Gorbals* was wonderful in the first part of the ballet, but she entirely missed the Madonna-like simplicity of the reformed girl in the last scenes. When she danced the role of the Betrayed Girl in *The Rake's Progress*, she made her seem like a waitress in a tea-shop, as one critic said. She began to get less and less of these parts, and very soon I began to get them myself.

All this time I had never once seen Sebastian. I knew he had come to London shortly after the Christmas holiday when I had left Bracken Hall so suddenly, because Caroline had told me so in her letters. He had got his scholarship to the Royal College of Music; had won prizes; had gone abroad to study. The music critics had already begun to sit up and take notice of Sebastian Scott. Caroline enclosed some of the Press notices in her letters: 'Clever young North Country composer conducts own symphony ... *The Lindisfarne Symphony*, by rising young musician ... brilliant score ... greatly influenced by his native moors, and rocky coastline ... atmosphere of wind-swept headlands, and wild, tossing seas ...'

Another review, in the *Musical Echo*, said: 'There is something very reminiscent of Tchaikovsky's ballet music in this young composer's work. I am not inferring – indeed far from it – that Mr Scott's music is in any way an imitation of the great Russian composer's, but merely draw attention to its strong balletic character – in this particular concerto, at any rate.'

There were Press photographs too. Sebastian in evening dress, baton in hand, conducting his own symphony. He looked older, of course, but his eyes still had their whimsical expression, his mouth its same arrogant twist. Many times I had gone to the Albert Hall in the hope of catching sight of him. Sometimes I had seen a close-cropped black head and thought it was Sebastian, but there had always been masses of people in the way, and I had never been able to get close enough to make sure.

Then came the wonderful day when I had sent the wire to Caroline as I had promised:

Odette-Odile in new production *Lac des Cygnes*. Will book seats for you all as arranged.

I managed to get five seats in the grand tier. They were for Aunt June, Uncle John, Fiona, and Caroline. The extra one was for Ian Frazer who was now Fiona's fiancé. They were to be married in the summer. I wrote and asked Caroline about Uncle Adrian, and she told me that he was in London, so he could get a seat for himself if he really wanted to see me dance. As for Sebastian – I pushed the thought of Sebastian firmly away from me. It was no use asking myself if *he* wanted to see me dance.

The great day arrived. There was a congratulatory telegram from Jonathan and Stella, who were living in Cornwall, and yet one more letter from Caroline, asking me to join them at their hotel after the performance, so that we could all have dinner together after the show.

In the morning I went round to the studio in Baker Street.

Most mornings now I went there to practise, and I felt that today of all days I must have my dear Madame Viret's encouragement.

'I feel terribly nervous,' I admitted when I had finished my work. 'I'm trembling even now. What on earth shall I be like when the time draws near?'

Madame spread her exquisite hands and shrugged her expressive shoulders.

'*Oh, là! là!* You weel be nervous, yes. Assuredly; what *artiste* ees not. You weel tremble in ze wings. You weel be white as a *pierce-neige* – a leetle snowdrop. But on ze stage – pouff! Ze audience – he ees not! You dance for yourself alone, and for your Prince in zis so beau-ti-ful ballet. You are lost in ze music – ze enchantment. Nevaire – nevaire 'ave you dance so well! I know eet 'ere.' Characteristically Madame laid her small white hands on her heart. 'Go, *ma mie*! I shall be there to watch. *Au revoir!*'

She kissed me on both cheeks, and I left the studio feeling a great deal calmer than I had done when I'd run up the stairs, reassured by Madame's faith in me.

At exactly half past twelve I crossed the road to the theatre, passed under the colonnade, and went round to the stage door. As usual, there was a little crowd of people waiting to see the principal dancers go in – those who were going to dance the leading roles – The Swan Queen, Prince Siegfried and the rest. With a shock I realized that today Odette, the Swan Queen, was going to be *me*. They were waiting for me!

'Well,' I thought, 'thank goodness they don't know me yet, even if they have seen me on the stage.'

But I rejoiced too soon! A small girl of about twelve, obviously from a dancing school, since she was whiling away the time by executing *entrechats* on the pavement, gave an excited shriek:

'*Mummy!* Look who it is! It's Miss Weston. You remember – Veronica Weston? We saw her in *The Ice Maiden* at

180

Sadler's Wells. And she was one of the Little Swans in *Swan Lake*, and we saw her in—'

At once the crowd surged respectfully towards me.

'Miss Weston – *would* you? ... Miss Weston, if you wouldn't mind ... Would it be an awful bother if? ... We simply *adored* your performance in *The Ice Maiden* ...' Autograph books popped out; much-read copies of popular books on ballet appeared from nowhere. Someone produced a linen teacloth with the autographs of famous ballet dancers embroidered all over it. Would I please sign here – no, just *here*. Yes, under Robert Helpmann.

'Gosh! Aren't you *tiny*!' exclaimed a large schoolgirl, with an envious sigh. 'And you're four years older than I am – yes. I read all about you in the *Dancing News*. You were eighteen last May.' She sighed again. 'No wonder you look like a fairy when you dance! What are you dancing this afternoon, Miss Weston?'

'I'm Odette-Odile in *Swan Lake*.' I answered.

There was a positive hush of awe.

'Odette? Golly! How wonderful! What a perfectly marvellous role to dance! What does it feel like to be dancing the Odette Odile role on Covent Garden stage, Miss Weston? Breathtaking, I expect?'

'I – don't know,' I faltered. 'You see, this afternoon is the very first time I've danced it, as a matter of fact.'

'Oh, *Mummy*!' said the small schoolchild, hopping up and down on one leg in an ecstacy of longing. 'Oh, Mummy, I *wish* we hadn't gone last night. Oh, I know it was Moira Shearer, and of course she's lovely, but I'd rather see Miss Weston – really, I would. You see, I feel we sort of know her now, Mummy—'

'It's no use, Jacinthe,' her mother said firmly. 'You know we weren't able to get seats for this afternoon, and in any case we couldn't possibly afford to go to the ballet twice running. Now don't be naughty, Jacinthe!'

'Look,' I put in quickly, seeing the child's downcast face,

'I'll send you a signed photograph of me in my Odette dress. I had one taken at rehearsal yesterday. How will that do, Jacinthe?'

The tears that were gathering in the child's eyes turned to smiles, and several people behind me murmured approving things.

'Why, she's just like a schoolgirl herself, so pale and young-looking, and not a *bit* stuck up!'

'Thank you!' I laughed. 'And now, if you'll excuse me, I really must go. It takes such ages to get ready.'

The crowd parted respectfully for me, and I slipped in through the stage door.

'Best of luck, miss!' George, the doorkeeper, yelled after me as I sped up the stairs to my dressing-room. 'You'll do well, I'm sure.'

'Thank you, George!' I yelled back.

When I opened the dressing-room door I saw at once that there was something unusual lying on my make-up table. It was a bunch of red roses, and on the card fastened to the stems of the flowers was the one word: 'Sebastian.'

Just that! No word of apology or good luck. I gave a wry smile. How like Sebastian! He hadn't a big, generous nature like Jonathan. He was brilliant, and witty, and arrogant. Above all, he was proud. No, he would certainly never utter one word of apology to me or to anyone else – I was quite sure of that. Still, he *had* sent me red roses, and my heart glowed. We were friends again, and he had meant me to know it.

But there was no time now for dreaming. Quickly, because I was already ten minutes late, I pulled on an old pair of practice tights, together with a pair of blocked shoes, and dashed down to the stage – Covent Garden stage, a ghostly place in the half-light; a place shadowy with the memories of all the great ones who had danced there. I could almost see their faces looking at me out of the wings, hear the rustle of their dresses, the tap of their shoes...

182

After I had warmed up I dashed back to my dressing-room, and began to dress. Swiftly I shed my workaday clothes, and with them my ordinary, workaday personality. I became an enchanted princess, a princess with no voice with which to plead her love, but only her large, dark, speaking eyes, her graceful arms, her dancing feet. The mirrored dressing-room threw back my image a dozen times as, with the help of my dresser, I bent this way and that, pulling up tights, fine as gossamer, settling my snowy *tutu*, putting last touches to my make-up. Behind Sebastian's roses my mirrored face looked back at me – eyes long-lashed and slanting; sleek, black hair framed in white swan feathers; slender shoulders rising from heart-shaped, satin bodice.

Now it was time for me to go down to the stage. With a last look round the quiet dressing-room, I shut the door behind me, never dreaming that I was leaving it for the last time as an unknown ballerina. Yes, that dressing-room was destined to look very different when I saw it again!

As I waited quietly in the wings, trembling slightly with nervousness, I knew that somewhere out there in the darkened auditorium Sebastian was waiting – waiting for me to appear. Long afterwards I learned that he'd seen me many times in my other roles; that night after night he'd sat in the gallery down at Sadler's Wells and watched me dance the Sugar Plum Fairy, the Odette solo, the solo from *Les Sylphides* – all the dances he'd seen me do in those far-off days in Northumberland. But I didn't know this now. All I knew now was that Sebastian had sent me red roses, that Sebastian had forgiven me.

And then came the haunting melody of Tchaikovsky's music. With a *pas de chat* I leaped gracefully into my position on the stage, ready for the famous mime scene with my partner, Prince Siegfried.

I have only a vague idea of what happened next. The lovely story unfolded itself, as with beautiful mimic gestures I told my Prince of my enchantment, besought him with my eyes to

The lovely story unfolded itself

rescue me. He swore to protect me, to shield me from evil. But alas! my Prince was deceived and became betrothed by mistake to the Magician's wicked daughter, Odile. I danced the difficult role of Odile as I had always known I should – flashing, brilliant, and cruel, keeping Prince Siegfried enthralled, never allowing his eyes to stray towards the window where his real, enchanted Princess stood, silhouetted, wringing her hands in despair. I heard the gasp of admiration from the watchers in the wings when I turned the thirty-two *fouettés*, making them look as easy as if I were running across the room.

As for the audience – I had completely forgotten it was there, until the thunderous applause broke forth and the curtain fell at the end of the last act, only to rise again while I curtsied this way and that, together with the rest of the Company. Then the other dancers disappeared, and Prince Siegfried and I were left to take a curtain alone.

But even this would not satisfy the audience. Curtain after curtain I took, whilst flowers were handed out of the wings and piled at my feet. The stage manager came to my side and made his bow, and then, miracle of miracles, suddenly Madame herself was there, holding my hand. In full view of the audience she kissed me on both cheeks.

The audience rose to its feet, and if it hadn't been an audience composed of ballet enthusiasts I'm sure it would have cheered! Then the noise ceased as if by magic. Madame was going to speak. Quietly, in her beautifully modulated voice, Madame introduced me as the youngest and newest *prima ballerina*, a worthy follower of Margot Fonteyn, Shearer, and the rest of that glittering company of Wells *artistes*.

'Here is Veronica,' said Madame, drawing me forward. 'Your own *ballerina*, whom you, yourselves, have acclaimed for her brilliant dancing this afternoon – Veronica, unheralded by the Press, totally unadvertised, until this afternoon, almost unknown. But I, and others connected with the Sadler's Wells Company, have watched Veronica's progress, and we all know how much she deserves her success.'

The thunderous applause broke out again. The audience would have me speak!

I stood hesitating, but before I could open my mouth, Prince Siegfried, who was my old friend Toni Rossini, was at my side. Quietly he addressed the waiting people.

'Dancers do not speak,' he told them, 'any more than flowers do. Veronica is very tired; she asks me to ask you if she may please go home.'

The curtain fell for the last time. People surged out of the wings to be the first to congratulate me. Never, it seemed, had there been such an enthusiastic audience at a matinée.

'Ah, Veronique – *mon petit chou*,' said a warm voice in my ear. 'Veronique, my leetle one – she 'as arrive'! I knew eet! Nevaire 'ave I seen such dancing!' It was dear Madame Viret – she who had helped me from the very beginning of my dancing career. Disheartened, tired, often sick at heart, I had gone to Madame's studio in Baker Street, and always I had left her refreshed and strengthened. Yes, I owed much of my success to dear Madame Viret.

'It was all due to you, Madame,' I said, tears in my eyes. 'I couldn't have done it without you; indeed I couldn't.'

Madame snapped her fingers.

'*Ah, ça!* Zat waz nozing zat I did – just one leetle finger in ze pie, as you say! I see you soon, my Veronique, yes?'

'Tomorrow, Madame,' I answered with raised voice, for already masses of people were crowding in upon me, and Madame's tiny figure was fast disappearing in the press.

'Felicitations, Veronique!' said Toni, pressing my hand. 'Today you were indeed beautiful. You have made my dream of you come true.'

'It's awfully nice of you to say so,' I answered. 'And thank you, Toni, for partnering me so wonderfully. I don't believe you ever thought of yourself at all!'

'Indeed, no, Veronique – no one could think of anyone else when you were there,' said Toni gallantly.

As I had foreseen long ago, Toni would never be remembered for his dancing. Yet the strange thing was that when he danced as my partner, people said that he was like another person – that his dancing reached heights that no one believed him capable of attaining.

When at last I escaped to my dressing-room, I found that it was full of people, too. They weren't stage people this time, but people from the outside world – girls who claimed to have known me before Daddy died, neighbours whom I didn't even remember. Suddenly I seemed to have an enormous number of friends!

They had brought up my flowers from the stage, and my once-bare dressing-room looked a cross between an expensive florist's and a conservatory. Sebastian's roses had been removed from my make-up table, and their place was now taken by a gilded basket of queer, bilious-looking green flowers with black markings that made them look as if they were in the last stages of decay.

'Orchids!' someone murmured with a grimace, adding with a glance at the card: 'From Oscar Deveraux – Irma Foster's husband. You know – the famous critic, my dear. Trust him to be there at the début of a new star! You've really arrived, Miss Weston, when Oscar Deveraux sends you flowers. He never makes a mistake.'

'No, he waits until everyone else is perfectly sure and have committed themselves; then dear Oscar jumps the queue!' said someone else nastily. 'You're right – no mistakes for Oscar!'

Quietly I removed the orchids and replaced Sebastian's roses on my table. If only – if only Sebastian were there himself. What would I give if all these strange people would only go away, and I could have my old friend, Sebastian, in their place.

'Please—' I begged. 'I'm most awfully tired. Would you mind if I changed now.'

After a long time the room emptied, the women taking a last

187

envious glance at my *tutu*, the men murmuring polite fare-wells. I was alone at last. All that remained of my triumph was the heavy scent of the flowers banked round the room and the haunting perfume left behind by my women admirers. Yes, and the thought of all the tomorrows – the glorious, unclouded tomorrows, when I would dance *Giselle, The Sleeping Beauty*, and all the other classic roles a dancer must make her own before she earns the title of *Prima Ballerina*.

Only one small cloud remained – Sebastian. I wanted to hear him say he'd forgiven me.

When my dresser had gone away, carrying my Swan Queen dress carefully on her arm, I removed the last of my make-up, and slipped into my outdoor things. In a very few minutes I stood ready to go. The mirrors reflected me as they had done when I had stood before them in all my stage finery. Now, my real self looked back at me – small, pale, childlike, only my narrow feet with their highly arched insteps showing that I was not the schoolgirl I seemed. The traces of make-up that had eluded me made my eyes seem even larger and darker than usual. They looked sad, I thought. I smiled suddenly, and dropped a curtsy to my reflection in the glass. Stupid to be sad just because a stiff-necked boy like Sebastian refused to be one of my crowd of admirers!

When I reached the stage door, I could see that there were a lot of people outside it, but not until the doorkeeper smiled down at me did it occur to me what they were waiting for.

'Hearty congrats, miss!' said George warmly. 'You deserve it, I'm sure. Big crowd outside, miss. Sure you'll be all right?'

My eyes widened.

'You mean?—'

'Waitin' for you, miss,' grinned George. ''Undreds of 'em! Autograph books galore! Take you hours to sign all that lot! Take my advice, miss, and slip out through the theatre. I'll get you a taxi in a trice, miss.'

I hesitated. Outside the stage door I could hear the news-boys shouting the evening papers:

'Late special! Late special! Scenes at Covent Garding! Unknown bally dancer leaps to fame! Late special!'

'Well – do you think I ought, George? Taxis are terribly expensive. You see – I've got a good way to go—'

George grinned again.

'Judging by the row in that there theatre this afternoon, miss, there ain't no more call for you to go counting your pennies! What address shall I say, miss?'

I gave him Mrs Crapper's address, for I intended to go home and change before dinner, and I could see him raising his eyebrows at it mentally.

'Righty-ho, miss! Hey – wait a minute, though! Know a young gent of the name of Scott, miss?'

My heart leaped, and a thrill of joy ran through me.

'Sebastian!' I cried. 'I should just think I do! Oh, yes – I know Sebastian Scott all right!'

'Well, he's waitin' art there in that crowd,' said George, nodding over his shoulder towards the stage door. 'Been inquiring for you, he has. I'll send him round to the main door, if you like, miss. Mebbe he's got a car of his own waitin'. He looked that sort of a young gent!'

In the dim vestibule I met Sebastian again for the first time since we'd quarrelled, all that long time ago. He was just the same – only a little graver and older.

'Veronica!' he said, and came forward with outstretched hands. 'Veronica, you were wonderful!'

Then he tipped up my face towards him.

'I once told you you were the nicest girl I'd ever met,' he went on softly. 'Well, I've met lots of girls since then, but I still think you're the nicest. I was going to kiss you goodbye that other time – remember? Well, I'm going to do it now, only it's not goodbye, Veronica!'

PICCOLO FICTION
Superb Stories – Popular Authors

FOLLYFOOT   Monica Dickens   20p
Based on the Yorkshire Television Series
FOXY   John Montgomery 20p
FOXY AND THE BADGERS   John Montgomery   20p
THE CHRISTMAS BOOK   Enid Blyton   20p
THE OTTER'S TALE   Gavin Maxwell   25p
The junior 'Ring of Bright Water'
THE STORY OF A RED DEER   J. W. Fortescue   20p
FREEWHEELERS   The Sign of the Beaver
  Alan Fennell 20p

PICCOLO NON-FICTION
The best in fun – for everyone

CODES AND SECRET WRITING   Herbert Zim   20p
JUNIOR COOK BOOK   Marguerite Patten   25p
BRAIN BOOSTERS   David Webster   20p
PICCOLO QUIZ BOOK   Tom Robinson   20p
FUN AND GAMES OUTDOORS   Jack Cox   20p
FUN-TASTIC   Denys Parsons   20p

PICCOLO
COLOUR BOOKS

Great new titles for boys and girls from eight to twelve. Fascinating full-colour pictures on every page. Intriguing, authentic easy-to-read facts.

DINOSAURS
SECRETS OF THE PAST
SCIENCE AND US
INSIDE THE EARTH
EXPLORING OTHER WORLDS
STORMS
SNAKES AND OTHER REPTILES
AIRBORNE ANIMALS

25p each   Fit your pocket – Suit your purse

PICCOLO FICTION
For younger readers

ALBERT AND HENRY   Alison Jezard   20p
ALBERT IN SCOTLAND   Alison Jezard   20p

These and other PICCOLO Books are obtainable from all booksellers and newsagents. If you have any difficulty please send purchase price plus 5p postage to P.O. Box 11, Falmouth, Cornwall.

While every effort is made to keep prices low it is sometimes necessary to increase prices at short notice. PAN Books reserve the right to show new retail prices on covers which may differ from those advertised in the text or elsewhere.